Sherlock Holmes
THE HACKNEY HORROR

William Meikle

Copyright William Meikle 2019
Cover Art by M Wayne Miller

I

The card that started the case arrived at some time on a Tuesday afternoon in the hottest August on record. It was several hours before I was apprised of its existence, for I was with a patient who had taken quite a turn for the worse in my rooms, and I had to see him settled before I could tend to the day's administrative tasks. Even after reading the card, it was several hours before I caught up with my required paperwork.

In the end, I did not even have the time to return home and change for the outing. I had a wash and shave at the hospital and then had to hurry across town to arrive in time for the occasion to which I had been invited—an evening performance in The Lyceum.

Given that the card had come from my good friend Sherlock Holmes, and knowing his tastes in matters of the stage, I expected to be attending a rather highbrow affair—a light opera perhaps, or a string quartet. I was rather taken aback to see the placard in the foyer for an evening of music-hall entertainment, it not being something that would normally attract Holmes' attention. I was also surprised to find that, despite my tardiness, our customary box was empty.

The ashtrays were still clear, which told me that Holmes had not yet arrived.

I assumed he had been diverted to another matter. Given that I was rather tired from a day at the hospital, and that I felt underdressed for the occasion, I considered taking my own leave. But I had nothing else planned for the evening, and as no further correspondence from my friend seemed to be forthcoming, I ordered myself a glass of brandy and settled down for the entertainment.

I soon began to regret my decision to stay, even after the most welcome arrival of the brandy, for the fare on show was shoddy stuff indeed.

The first singer, a pleasing-to-the-eye soprano, got everything off to a steady but far from spectacular start, but the next act up, a portly Scottish comedian, badly misread the mood of the crowd with a string of jokes at the expense of the inhabitants of London. His material might have gone down well in Sauchiehall Street in his hometown, but down in the Strand he was dead and buried before he realized it. They were baying for his blood by the time he beat an ignominious retreat a mere five minutes later.

Things went downhill sharply from there, in a succession of dull magicians, feats of strength and agility that showed precious few signs of either quality, and a quartet of singers so badly out of tune that at first I thought they were another comedy act.

After that assault on our ears, the crowd was restless, and I sensed trouble brewing, so I was feeling nervous on behalf of the next performer before he even reached center stage. The stooped gait and shuffling walk of the man who came on did little for my confidence.

Several boos rang out, and a cry of 'Show us your knickers, mate,' got a big laugh. I thought the performer might immediately wilt under the pressure, but his voice carried clear through the whole auditorium when he spoke, and it rang with an air of confidence that caused the audience to at least start to pay attention to what he had to say.

"My name is John Green," he began, his accent clearly local, which immediately gave him a better start than the Scotsman had. His speech was overlaid with the signs of an educated, if not exactly cultured, upbringing, and was free from the harsh nasal quality often associated with the area.

"I was lucky enough to be born with a remarkable brain," he continued. "One that I have trained and honed to a perfect instrument through years of dedication."

"Go and hone yourself," a wag in the audience shouted, amid much hilarity. It did not break the man's composure.

"I have filled my mind with a veritable encyclopedia of facts and figures, alongside much of the great literature of history, including the whole of the Bible, both Old and New Testaments."

"Pride cometh before a fall," a voice shouted out from the audience, and that got a laugh all round.

"Actually, the quotation is more accurately depicted as 'Pride goes before destruction, a haughty spirit before a fall.' Proverbs, chapter sixteen, verse eighteen. Ask me another."

A smattering of applause ran through the crowd—they were starting to warm to the man. And he too seemed to be warming to the task. He walked to the front of the stage and raised his voice.

"I am willing to put my money where my mouth is. If you ask me a question of a factual nature and I do not know the answer, I will give you a sixpence for your trouble."

"Let's see your money, pal."

Mr. Green jingled his trouser pocket. Coins rattled and the man smiled.

"I've got something in here for the ladies too, and it ain't small change."

That earned the best laugh of the night thus far, and Mr.

Green's act was off and running. Over the course of the next ten minutes, the crowd threw a series of questions at him; some mundane, some outlandish. He displayed that he had not been boasting—he did indeed have a prodigious number of facts at his fingertips. He was also, as he relaxed, looking strangely familiar to me, and I realized why Holmes was not in the box beside me. As yet, he had not had to take a single sixpence from his pocket, but I believed I might have a question that would test him.

I was to be thwarted in my plans. A theater attendant came into the box and handed me a note. It was a hand I recognized immediately, and it was brief and to the point.

"Meet me in Green's dressing room after the act. And be careful—there could be trouble. H."

I decided to act immediately, and therefore I missed the climax of the act, but as I went backstage, I heard the roar of approval and a deafening chorus of applause. Mr. Green was the star of the show. He arrived at the dressing-room door at the same time as I did, and smiled. Up close, there was no mistaking him.

"Well, Watson," Holmes said, slipping into his normal cultured voice. "How did I do?"

"Remarkably well," I replied. "But I would have had you with my question, given the chance."

If I expected him to rise to the bait, I was to be disappointed. He pushed open the dressing room door and bundled me inside before stripping off the wig and rubbing away the face paint. By now I myself had quite forgotten about any question I might have asked him on stage, for there was a bigger question lying on the floor of the dressing room.

A man—the real Mr. Green, I supposed—lay in a fetal curl on a threadbare rug. I bent to check on him, but it was immediately obvious that he was quite dead.

"No time to explain, Watson," Holmes said. "Watch the door. If it is anyone but Lestrade, do not let them enter."

As I moved to the door, he went to bend over the body where he started his customary minute observance of every tiny detail. From outside the door I heard a piano player lead the crowd in a chorus of a popular song of the day, but there was no sound of anyone approaching along the corridor. I chanced a look, opening the door by an inch or so to peer out. The corridor was empty.

"Close the door," Holmes said. "I may have bought us some time with my little deception, but equally, I may have forced their hand. They may make another attempt on Mr. Green's life at any moment."

"But Holmes, the man is already quite dead."

Holmes stood from the body and looked me in the eye.

"Yes, Watson. But they do not know that. With any luck, my play-acting will convince them that they have failed in their first attempt and will flush them out into the light."

"Who?" I asked. I had not yet caught up with what was happening and felt quite lost.

Holmes smiled grimly.

"That is what I am hoping to discover."

Seconds later I heard heavy footsteps in the corridor and I sensed a certain tension in Holmes' stance, as if he expected trouble, but the voice that called out was more than familiar enough to both of us.

"Holmes? If this is another of your blasted tricks, I'll …"

I opened the door to Inspector Lestrade of Scotland Yard. He stopped shouting as soon as he saw the body on the floor.

"Get in here," Holmes said. "And close the door behind

you."

A younger officer I did not know came in behind Lestrade. With all of us inside, the small dressing room seemed even smaller and more cramped.

"No games, Holmes," Lestrade said as he knelt to check the body. "I want a full account of what has happened here."

"And you will get one, Inspector," Holmes replied. "But first things first—would you like to catch the killer or not?"

Lestrade seemed on the verge of a snappy response when Holmes put a finger to his lips, asking for silence. We heard the audience laugh loudly out in the theater, and then once again there was the unmistakable sound of heavy footsteps in the corridor.

"Leave this to us, Holmes," Lestrade whispered.

The footsteps came closer, and then stopped—someone stood just on the other side of the door. The sound from the theater died to little more than a distant whisper and then rose again to a loud roar of applause. Whoever was outside had been waiting for the sound to cover what came next; the door banged open as if someone had put a shoulder into it. At the same instant the lamps in the room extinguished in a sudden gust of wind, leaving us in darkness that quickly became a chaotic mêlée of thrown punches, kicks and some rather exotic cursing from Lestrade. I lashed out at a large shadow, and immediately recoiled as my fist met something as hard as iron and just as unyielding. Someone grunted in pain, and I heard a loud crack that I knew immediately signaled a broken bone.

Then all fell silent.

"No one move," Holmes said.

A match sparked, and I saw Holmes' face, lit in flickering red and as solemn as I have ever seen him. He lit a lamp and illuminated the room. Lestrade sat on the floor sporting a bump on his forehead that would be a most impressive bruise later and the young officer stood, ghost-faced, nursing an arm that hung at an unnatural angle from the elbow.

There was no body on the floor and no sign of our assailant. Wherever he had gone, he had taken Mr. Green with him.

Holmes dashed out into the corridor—I merely had time to see that the gas lamps out there had also been extinguished before I turned my ministrations to the young policeman. Lestrade got to his feet, somewhat groggily, but refusing any aid.

"What in blazes just happened, Watson?"

I had no answer for him. Holmes returned in the doorway.

"He is gone, and there is no trail to follow, I'm afraid," he said. "Although how he managed it, I am at quite a loss to say."

"This lad needs a hospital," I said, having to hold the young officer upright to keep him from falling into a dead faint.

Holmes nodded.

"Let us see to that immediately." He turned to the Inspector. "You look like you could do with a drink, Lestrade. Let us return to Baker Street and sample some of Mrs. Hudson's fine brandy. I believe I owe you an explanation."

2

We arrived back in the Baker Street apartment sometime after ten, having taken time to get the young officer the medical attention he required. On another night I might have stayed by him to ensure he was comfortable, but I had left him in good hands, and my curiosity had been piqued—I wanted to hear how Holmes, and the rest of us, had become involved in this most perplexing matter.

By ten after the hour we were sitting in armchairs around the fireplace in the parlor. It was still too warm an evening to have a fire going in the grate, and even with the windows closed against the stifling fumes of the city outside, it was still a muggy, slightly unpleasant atmosphere. We proceeded to add tobacco smoke to the fug, and Holmes himself charged three large snifters of brandy before we settled to hear his tale.

"As you have probably surmised, it was no coincidence that I was at the theater tonight. I first met John Green in this very room, just after Christmas last year," he started. "He came to me with—shall we call it a filing problem? He wanted a new way to order some of the information he had stored as it was becoming rather unwieldy for him to process.

"I quickly discovered that he had a truly remarkable mind—one capable of retaining every scrap of information he either read, saw or heard. The storage of it all was not the problem—as you have often heard me say, the normal human mind is a vast expanse of empty space waiting to be filled. But as I said, Mr. Green was having problems with retrieval, having failed to adequately categorize the facts he was gathering—facts that were rapidly piling up in a jumble too tangled for him to unravel.

"I helped where I thought I could do him the most good. I had also quickly determined that despite the unique nature of his gift, Mr. Green was not a deep thinker and seemed unable or unwilling to make any connections between the disparate items he was so assiduously gathering.

"We had three sessions in all over the next week. I even went so far as to partake of one of his performances, so as to obtain a better idea of the uses to which he put his storeroom, but I did not see him again until this very evening.

"A card came this morning."

Holmes took a small rectangular card from his waistcoat pocket and passed it to me. On one side it had Green's name, and an address in Hackney. On the other was a scrawled script, written either by someone unaccustomed to the pen, or in some degree of haste.

Please meet me at the Lyceum tonight. I fear for my life.

I showed the card to Lestrade, who merely grunted and sipped more brandy.

"Of course," Holmes continued. "I could not in all honesty refuse such a plea. I booked our usual box, sent Watson a message, and made my way to the theater to arrive before the start of the show, hoping to talk to the man before he went onstage.

"But even by arriving early, I was too late for Mr. Green. He lay as you both saw him, on the floor of his dressing room, quite dead. A cursory glance at the body told me little I did not already know, and when there was a knock on the door, and a shout announced 'Five minutes Mr. Green,' I decided on my plan to try to draw the killer out.

"As Watson knows, I am rather handy with stage makeup and am capable of disguises that can fool the casual observer. I took Green's place on stage—and even if I do say so myself, gave a performance that managed to persuade everyone present that John Green was still very much alive. When I returned from the auditorium, Watson met me at the door—and the rest you know."

"I know dashed little," Lestrade said. "How was the man killed—if indeed he was even dead in the first place?"

"Of course he was dead," Holmes replied. "You have my word on it."

"All right, then—he was dead. So how did he disappear from under our noses the way he did? I'd bet my pension there was only one man who came into the darkened room—he was a big chap, I'll give you that, but not big enough to have off with a body too quickly for us to catch him in the act."

Holmes sat back in his chair and sucked at his cheroot for long seconds before answering.

"I have been asking myself that same question, Inspector," he said. "And as yet I do not have an answer for you. But I will."

Lestrade polished off the brandy in one gulp and stood.

"Well, until you do, Mr. Holmes, I ain't about to do anything official in this matter. We've got a man—a body—missing: that's all we know at the moment. There's an assault on a police officer to consider, of course, but we have no suspects to talk to, and no leads to follow, if I understand you right?"

"Only a most tenuous thread at the moment, Inspector."

"Well, then," Lestrade replied. "Let me know when you find someone I can repay for this bump, and I'll come running. Until then …"

He left us sitting by the fireplace.

Holmes sat quietly for so long I thought he was pondering the problem. I contented myself with having another snifter and lighting up a fresh pipe. He surprised me by speaking, just after I had gotten the bowl lit to my satisfaction.

"What would your question have been, Watson?" he said.

"Please do not tell me you've been fretting on that? What's the matter, Holmes—are you afraid I might have stumped you?"

Holmes smiled.

"You know me better than anyone else in London," he said. "If anyone were to get the better of me, I would expect it to be you."

"Well, then, I shall leave you guessing," I replied. "And it will warm the cockles of my heart on cold winter nights to know that I have at least bested you once."

3

I retired to bed around midnight, leaving Holmes sitting by the fireplace. He was still there when I rose in the morning. Holmes has a remarkable ability to focus his mental effort and bend it for long periods where he almost seems to be in a trance, or even asleep. I have seen him sit upright in that same armchair for ten hours at a stretch with nary a flicker of an eyelid to show that he was still conscious. He often emerged from these sessions physically tired, as after a long energetic walk, and this time was no different.

His eyes opened, and he stared straight at me for several seconds before I saw recognition there.

"Be so kind as to ask Mrs. Hudson to prepare a light breakfast, Watson," he said. "We need to be out and about this morning—and soon, too, if we are to make some headway on this case."

That was all he said before rising and tending to his ablutions. I did as I was bid and went downstairs where Mrs. Hudson was bustling around her kitchen. I passed on Holmes' request for a light breakfast. She waved me away.

"He'll have bacon and eggs, and like it—I have nothing else at hand. It's this weather, you see? None of the shops has anything fresh at all. I remember when …"

I beat a hasty retreat—when a landlady of a certain age uses those three words it is best to plead a prior engagement, otherwise you might still be listening to her story by

Christmas. When I returned upstairs to the apartment, Holmes was back in the armchair again, puffing contentedly on a fresh pipe.

"Well, Watson," he said, "it seems we have a genuine mystery on our hands. I have examined all the details from several angles and have not yet come to any firm understanding. I will say this, though—I believe Mr. Green saw something he was not meant to see—and for that, he was killed by persons as yet unknown to us. Today, we shall attempt to shed some light into the darker corners."

Mrs. Hudson arrived to put out breakfast—she was as good as her word, laying a table of eggs, bacon, toast and enough of her fine marmalade to disguise any staleness in the bread itself. Holmes took to it with gusto despite his earlier request for a light meal, and after two cups of strong, sweet tea, professed himself ready for action.

I barely had time to collect my service pistol from my room before Holmes shepherded me out into Baker Street.

If anything, it was already even warmer than the previous day; an oppressive, stifling humidity that sapped the strength from a man and enhanced the stench of a city that seemed to be rotting under the heat. If I had thought the shade inside a cab might help, I was immediately proved wrong. Our thankfully short journey to the Lyceum in the Strand brought back to mind some of my less-memorable days in India during the monsoon, and I was soaked with perspiration as we alighted outside the theater. Holmes looked as annoyingly cool and dapper as ever, having barely broken a sweat.

"Come on, Watson. I believe we left here too hastily last night. I must see Green's room before too many others have trampled through it."

Fortunately the theater interior proved to be an oasis of darkness and cooler air, and I quickly forgot the discomfort of the journey as anticipation grew. Holmes had the air of a man on the hunt and as ever I was only too happy to follow.

The theater seemed to be empty save for a single cleaning lady up on the stage brushing away last night's sawdust. She paid us no attention as we made our way quickly backstage and into Green's dressing room.

To my eye it looked exactly as we had left it. There had been no attempt to repair the broken door; a chair lay on its side where it had fallen during the scuffle in the dark; and the jars and bottles of stage make-up sat undisturbed on the dressing table. Holmes ignored all of these and made straight for a china teacup on the table.

"This was still warm when I arrived yesterday evening," he said. "Had I had more time I might have paid more attention to that fact."

He sniffed at the contents of the cup.

"A South China blend," he said. "And rather unpleasant. But there's something else there, an odor I cannot identify. I do believe Mr. Green might have been poisoned."

He took a small glass phial from his pocket and carefully poured the cup's contents into it, sealing it with a rubber stopper. He held it up to the light. It looked golden, almost glowing. He studied it for a few more seconds, and then put the phial away in his waistcoat pocket.

"I have a bad feeling about this, Holmes," I said. "There's more to this case than meets the eye—I can feel it in my water."

Holmes laughed.

"Much as I admire your instincts, Watson, you will forgive me if I trust to my methods."

With no further ado, he got down on his hands and knees and began a painstaking search of the floor and rug, starting in the area where Green's body had been and working outward in tight circles. I knew better than to disturb him in this activity, and to try to help would only earn me an admonishment for meddling, so I went back out into the corridor, lit up a cheroot, and prepared myself for a wait.

My recollection of the struggle in the dark room was only of vague shapes and shadows; that, and a bruise on my knuckles, was all I had to show for the encounter. But as I stood there in the theater corridor and looked left and right, I realized one thing. Whoever had taken Green's body had to have been both strong and quick to make it along the length of the passage and not be seen by Holmes when he left the room in pursuit no more than five seconds later.

I was almost finished with my second cheroot before Holmes pronounced himself satisfied with his search.

"Lestrade has been to that bar in Whitechapel again; Mr. Green is—or was—fond of long walks in muddy conditions somewhere outside the city; and there is a strange tang where our intruder put his feet—faint but unmistakable, and as yet I cannot place it. It may be no more than that he stepped in a spillage of vinegar, or it may be something more pertinent. I need more facts, Watson. And to obtain them, I am afraid we shall now have to go to Hackney."

4

The trip to Hackney proved every bit as uncomfortable as I had expected, despite the fact that Holmes paid extra for haste, which at least afforded us a breeze, albeit a warm one.

Holmes had given the carriage driver the card containing Green's address. At first I was not sure he would agree to take us; it was a long trip for a central London driver—and there was something else bothering the man, something that only became apparent after he had read the actual address.

"Them's not safe parts to be around, sirs," he said. "Not for gentlemen like yourselves. You hear stories in my line of work—foreigners, or so I've heard. That area is full of black-hearted sailing men that'll slit your throat for a groat."

I showed the man my service pistol.

"We can take care of ourselves—and you, for that matter."

"As long as we're out of there afore dark," was the last thing the driver said as we set off. "Ain't no way I'm waiting around for you after the sun's down."

Holmes assured him that we intended to be back in town for an early supper, and that mollified the man somewhat. But it seemed that Holmes' request for haste was unnecessary—the man drove as if the hounds of hell themselves were at his heels. This was not a great problem while we were on the maintained streets in town, but once past Euston the carriage rocked and swayed as we hit ruts and holes. By the time we disembarked I was feeling more than a little shaken and slightly queasy.

"The street you want is over there a-ways, sirs," the driver said, pointing past a row of cottages that had seen better days. "You can't miss it—if you reach the old church, you've gone too far. I'll just wait here for you. Shall we say an hour? And if you're not back, I won't be responsible for what happens."

Holmes assured the man that we would indeed return in plenty of time, and offered him a handsome bonus if he would be as good as his word and stay. I was not so sure it would be enough, for I had seen the look in the man's eyes. It wasn't just a driver's normal reluctance to go beyond his usual territory—this was more akin to stark terror.

I remarked on the fact to Holmes as we walked past the cottages and into the road where Green lived.

"I saw that too, Watson," he replied. He looked around. "Maybe he has seen this street before."

It was only then that I paid attention to our surroundings.

I have had the misfortune to visit many poor communities both in my years in the Army and in tending to the sick in the sprawling chaos that is London, but I have rarely seen a more squalid, degenerate sight than that which met us in Hackney.

The street—a loose term in this case—was obviously one of the oldest still extant in the modern city, being mainly black-and-white-timbered exteriors beneath dingy thatched roofs. The road was packed earth and rough gravel, with no pavement to speak of. Rubbish and sewage lay strewn in the dirt; barefoot children danced in it as if it were paved in gold. Only one in every four of the buildings looked inhabited, and of the others, some had fallen in on themselves, yet more had obviously been burned to the ground, and one had a tall birch tree growing up through the thatch, although even that was twisted and stunted. There was only a small huddle of adults in view, and none showed any sign of desiring conversation—indeed, they pointedly turned their backs on us as we walked up the narrow thoroughfare.

The heat was even more oppressive here, so much so that the haze caused the view ahead of us to waver and flow like a fever dream. Our destination would be, according to what few house numbers we could find, at the far end, an area dominated by a squat stone church of a great age that faced the length of the street. The closer we came to that building, the fewer people we saw out and about—no children played, and there was no sign of the stray dogs that seemed to plague the lower reaches of the road. A sweltering dampness wrapped us like a wet blanket as the heat became almost unbearable. I was very glad when Holmes turned off the road and rapped, hard, on the door of number 23—the Green residence.

An elderly lady—or so I thought—answered the door. I took her for Green's mother, as she was as bent and wizened as the trees outside; she barely came up to the height of my chest and moved like someone beset with back pains over a long spell of years.

I got a better look at her as we were welcomed inside the house, and I had to revise my first opinion—she was little older than I, but had been stricken by either weariness or illness and had aged before her time. Her eyes seemed bright and clear enough as she studied our faces.

"Have you seen my John?" she asked. "Only he didn't come home last night, see—and my John always comes home."

She led us into a parlor that belied the poverty and squalor outside, being well appointed with fine, if aged, pieces of furniture, all kept spotlessly free of dust.

"You're that Sherlock Holmes fella, ain't you?" she said. "John told me all about you—putting ideas into his head. It wouldn't surprise me if this isn't all your fault."

It certainly surprised Holmes.

"What do you mean, madam?"

"Oh, madam, is it?" She jabbed out a finger, poking Holmes sharply in the chest. "I'll give you 'madam' if my John has come to any harm."

Holmes, unable to deal with a lady in that state of mind, left her to me. I managed to persuade her to sit down, and mollified her somewhat by offering her a smoke. She took to it with the gusto of a seasoned practitioner.

"John was happy till he met you," she said to Sherlock. "Doing his shows and bringing home good money. Then you went and told him about how you connect things, one to another. It ruined him, that did. He spent hours making up stories trying to make things join up with other things. Tried to explain it all to me once, but it fair made my head hurt so I told him to stop, After that he took to taking walks out past the church. He said it cleared his head, said it helped him with his palace—that's what he called it, after seeing you. Filled his head with more nonsense; that's all it did. Then he came back from a walk early yesterday morning, all excited-like. Said he'd found something that even Sherlock Holmes won't have spotted. And that were I last I saw of him."

It had all come out of her in a rush, and the act seemed to drain the life from her, She slumped back in her chair, tears running down her cheeks.

"He didn't come home last night, see—and my John always comes home."

I leaned forward, intending to tell her—as gently as I

could manage—that her husband would never be coming home, but Holmes put a hand on my arm.

"Inspector Lestrade of Scotland Yard is even now looking for your husband," Holmes said. It wasn't quite a lie, but it was hardly the truth, and I was not happy in its telling, but I had to admit it seemed to mollify the lady somewhat.

"You'll tell him to come home, won't you?" she said, her voice soft and low. Fresh tears were not far from the surface.

"Can you tell us," Holmes asked, "what you think he found on his walk? What set him off?"

Unfortunately, that was exactly the wrong question.

"Set him off? That were you—you and your hoity-toity ideas. My John were fine afore he met you." She started to rise out of the chair, but then had to sit back down, the exertion too much for her. "Now get out of my house. You're not wanted here."

We beat a cautious retreat, but she had a parting shout for us as we reached the door.

"Don't come back unless you've found my John—I've an axe out the back I keep for firewood, but it works just as well on heads."

Holmes made straight for the churchyard on leaving the house.

"I told you, Watson," he said. "Green saw something he shouldn't have—and it got him killed. Let us see if we can arrive at the bottom of it."

We were to be disappointed. The church was exactly what it seemed—a sad ruin that had once been full of worship and joy now tumbled into rubble and dust. What few patches of stained glass remained told of a wealthy history, but the interior was little more than a muddle of broken pews arranged in front of a stone altar whose great antiquity was obvious, even in the little light that penetrated inside. The extensive cemetery to the rear looked out over the expanse of what had been Hackney Marshes and was now one of the largest areas of open grassland in London. A muddy river meandered at a snail's pace nearby, and the only things moving apart from us were swarms of black flies. The whole place had an air of sullen morbidity that did not sit well with me at all.

Holmes strode around the building, studying it at length.

"I see nothing that might have piqued Green's interest," he finally admitted, before setting off through the graveyard.

Like the church itself, the stones were of considerable age, many going back to the seventeenth century and others looking even older, although they were so eroded by time and weather as to make the inscriptions illegible. Matted grass, briar and hawthorn ran rampant everywhere, making access to some parts of the cemetery hard going indeed, but Holmes pushed on, even to the extent of having his trouser legs ripped and torn by thorns.

After twenty minutes of this, he finally admitted defeat and we returned at a slow walk to the front of the church. We were ten yards from the building when Holmes stopped and sniffed.

"Do you smell it, Watson?"

"You know me, old man—unless it's burnt or burning I do not smell much of anything—too much boxing and not enough keeping my guard up, I'm afraid."

He hushed me to silence and sniffed again.

"It is gone now, but it was there—the same tang I smelled in Green's dressing room. The answer is here somewhere. It has to be."

It was only that that I noticed the light was going.

"We had best be leaving, Holmes," I said. "The driver will not wait, and it is a long walk to Baker Street."

Holmes had another look around. His head jerked back to one of the church windows; then he pointedly looked back at me.

"I think you are right, Watson," he said, loudly, as if wanting anyone in range to hear. "We shall return to Baker Street and see if we can ascertain what manner of poison did for Mr. Green."

He took my elbow and almost frog-marched me away.

"Do not look back," he whispered. "We are being watched. Let us see if they take the bait."

5

To my great surprise, the carriage driver had been as good as his word and waited for us, although he appeared eager to be on his way.

"Jump in, gents. It's time to go."

Holmes had a quick look round to see if anyone was watching our departure, and then we were off and flying back to Baker Street with the same inordinate haste with which we had come. Holmes leaned out to check behind us at each turn and junction, but shook his head each time—it seemed we had not been followed.

Once back in Baker Street, the cabbie pocketed Holmes' money quickly and doffed his cap.

"Many thanks, gents. I won't be making that trip again in a hurry. I'm off for a few pints of porter to wash the taste of the place from my mouth. If you have any sense, you'll do the same."

The carriage clattered away towards Paddington.

"Actually, Holmes, that is not a bad idea ..."

Holmes once again took my elbow and marched me inside.

"We will need clear heads. If I am right, we will have a visitor before this night is out."

We spent the evening in the Baker Street apartment at Holmes' workbench, applying a variety of tests to the sample that had been taken from the teacup in Green's dressing room.

"I may have been a trifle hasty in my assessment of Green's death, Watson," Holmes said just after the tall clock struck nine. I sat back from my so-far-fruitless study of the fluid to hear what he had to say. "It is partly a toxin of sorts. I believe it to be similar to an extract from jimson weed, one of the milder forms of nightshade."

"*Datura stramonium*?" I replied. "Yes, I can see the basis for your speculation. But that is primarily a hallucinogen, is it not?"

"In China, I believe it to also be used as an analgesic, to render patients unconscious during surgery."

I nodded, "I have heard of that on my travels. But that still does not explain the fact that the man was as dead as anyone I've seen."

"That is why I said that the *Datura* was only partly responsible. There is some other chemistry at work here that I cannot yet fathom. But as I said, we may have been premature in our assessment—I believe there is a good chance that John Green is still alive."

Shortly after ten, Holmes had me turn out the lamps, and we sat in darkness by the fireplace, the only light coming from the flare of tobacco in our pipes as we puffed.

"There was definitely someone in the church watching us? You are sure?"

"I'm sure, Watson. Just as I am sure that they will want to know what we have discovered about their poison. Now, quiet—we do not want to scare them off."

We sat there as the city went silent—or as silent as it ever became. The rumble of carriages in the street diminished from a constant noise to only one every few minutes, and we heard the occasional murmur of subdued conversation from the pavement beneath the open window. Mrs. Hudson went to bed, as regular as the tall clock itself, on the stroke of eleven.

Holmes retreated into his shell of concentration. I did not have his mental resources, and I admonished myself for not at least having a glass of Scotch at hand to ease the boredom of our vigil. After what seemed an interminable time, the clock struck midnight. I moved slightly in my chair, intending to fill a fresh pipe. At that very moment, a darker shadow crossed the main window and I heard the slight scrape and rustle of someone pulling themselves inside. Had we been abed rather than by the fireplace, he would have been in and out, and we would have been none the wiser. He made his way to the workbench, as quiet as a cat on a hunt. There was another scrape and the flare of a struck match as he searched the contents of the table. It was only when he struck a second that Holmes leapt from his chair, taking advantage of the burst of flame to jump across the room and grab the intruder.

"Quick, Watson," he shouted. "We need some light on the matter."

I did the best I could while Holmes and the burglar scuffled behind me. Finally, after much fumbling in the dark, I lit the lamp and turned, just in time to see Holmes floor his opponent with a perfect left jab to the chin.

I walked over to help lift the man into a chair. Holmes had me tie him securely, hands behind the slats, before lifting the lamp from the table. He leaned in close to examine our captive.

"I thought I might know you," Holmes said as the man's eyes came back into focus. "But you are a stranger to me—you are not one of the city's petty thieves, at any rate. So tell me— who are you, and who has sent you here?"

I went round and lit up the other lamps in the room. The

man squinted against the sudden brightness, but showed no sign of answering Holmes' question. Holmes smiled, pulled up a chair and sat down opposite. He took his time lighting a pipe before speaking again.

"I would remind you that I am a personal friend of Inspector Lestrade of Scotland Yard," he started. "But even though that would be enough to ensure you three years in Pentonville, I can see that you are determined not to talk. So let me tell you what you have already told me."

All I saw was a slightly disheveled man in cheap working clothes, but I knew Holmes' methods, and tried to look more closely. As always, Holmes saw more than I could—more than any man would.

"You were the one watching us in Hackney today. There is no sense in denying that fact, as the stone dust at your knees and shoulders shows where you leaned against the walls of the old church—a most distinctive schist I have rarely seen this far south. You work in a coal-yard—that much is plain from your fingernails—but honest toil is not enough for you, so you have turned to crime. You are not, however, accustomed to this line of work; otherwise, you would not have been so easily fooled by our ruse of merely sitting in the dark and waiting for you, so the logical deduction is that you were either paid for or persuaded into this petty burglary. Tell me—did you take the ring off at home, or is it in your waistcoat pocket? The mark of the band is plain against the coal dust."

The man still hadn't spoken and showed no signs of doing so.

Holmes leaned forward and, with nimble fingers, made a quick search of the man's waistcoat pockets. It was no surprise to me that he did indeed retrieve a ring. I was too far away to see any detail, but it was gold and chunky, and not at all the kind of adornment I would expect the man before us to favor.

Holmes held the ring up to the light. The man twitched for the first time since we put him in the chair, but still didn't speak.

"So the ring is more important than your personal freedom?" Holmes said softly. "That is interesting. What is also interesting is this ring itself." Holmes threw it to me. It felt heavy in my hand. "I have seen such things on the fingers of our Masonic brethren. But this is something new to me."

The main device on the broad outward face of the ring was of a lion rampant—which made me consider a Scottish origin—but on closer examination the face pivoted on a cunning swivel and turned under my finger. If Holmes had not already inferred otherwise, I might have expected to see the square and compasses, but this was something entirely different.

The surface seemed to be jet, or some equally dark stone, inlaid with silver streaks, the workmanship being of the finest quality. Lines of various length radiated out from a central point which containing a small but most brilliant diamond, one that seemed to gleam with its own internal light. It drew me in, enticing me to look deeper into its heart. I came over slightly faint, as if something sucked at my very life force, and indeed I might have succumbed completely had Holmes not spoken up rather sharply at just that moment.

"Well, Watson," Holmes said. "What do you make of it? Is it anything you have come across on your travels in foreign climes?"

I turned the ring back so that the lion rampant was once again facing outward and any influence it might have had on me faded as quickly as it had come. I threw the ring back to Holmes; in truth I was glad to be rid of the thing.

"No idea, old man," I replied. "But there are certain Far Eastern cults …"

Holmes nodded.

"I believe you are on the right track. Our man here worships at no Christian altar."

Something thudded on the roof above us. We are occasionally plagued with dancing pigeons—a necessary evil when dwelling in the city, but if this was a pigeon, it was a jolly big one. And pigeons do not tend to bring immediate terror to the face of a man who had not so much as blinked at being tied to a chair.

"I ain't saying nothing," the man whispered, his first words since entering. He repeated them, shouting, as if needing someone to hear of his loyalty. "I ain't saying nothing."

A strange vibration filled the room, starting as a deep, not unpleasant hum that quickly rose in pitch to a high whine. Holmes' old violin rang in sympathy just before the glass face of the long clock cracked from top to bottom. I was driven to my knees, fearing my head would burst under the pressure. I turned towards Holmes but instead found my gaze drawn to the man in the chair. His eyes bulged, straining in their sockets, and blood showed at nostrils, lips and ears, just before his head slumped forward and the vibration cut off, leaving us once again in silence.

By the time I managed to stand and check on our captive, he was dead.

Holmes had not waited for my prognosis. He left at a run and I heard his footsteps clang on the iron fire stairs that led out onto our roof above me.

I followed at a more sedate pace and found him standing on the empty rooftop looking over the city.

"That's twice he has been too fast for me, Watson. It will not happen a third time."

As we turned to go back downstairs, Holmes stopped and tugged at my arm.

"There, Watson, do you smell it?"

And this time I did—a taint of acid, like vinegar in the nostrils.

6

Lestrade was not at all impressed at being summoned in the early hours of the morning—even less so to find a dead man bound to a chair in our rooms.

"By rights I should have the bleeding pair of you locked up for this," was the mildest of his many utterances as his men took our statements and the police doctor confirmed my diagnosis—an internal hemorrhage of the brain.

"It's hard to say," the young doctor said as he finally stood back. "But it looks almost as if his brains have been turned to liquid."

After all the hubbub died down—and after we had administered some medicinal Scotch to Mrs. Hudson in enough quantities to put her back to sleep—Holmes, Lestrade and I once again sat around the fireplace. Holmes gave Lestrade most—but not quite all—of the story.

"You think this has something to do with Green's disappearance?" Lestrade asked. He puffed on a pipe—the offer of a pouch full of Holmes' best Turkish blend had mollified him considerably after his earlier belligerence.

Holmes nodded. He showed Lestrade the ring and turned the face to the strange sigil on the inside.

"Have you seen anything like this before?"

Lestrade bent forward and studied the ring, so intent that I thought he, like myself, had fallen under some kind of charm. It was only after Holmes turned the face back to the lion rampant that the Inspector blinked, as if waking from sleep.

"Can't say as I have, Mr. Holmes," he said. "Some kind of a secret society, do you think?"

"Or a cult," Holmes said seriously. "This may be bigger than I first thought."

"And you never saw the man before?" Lestrade asked, looking first at Holmes and then at me.

"Never before today—although it is no coincidence that we were visiting Green's house when we were first spotted. Green saw something—I am now more sure of it than ever."

We sat, the three of us, going over and over what we knew so far, but even Holmes professed himself at a loss as to why the man might attempt to burgle us, or what he might have been after.

By the time Lestrade took his leave the first light of dawn was growing in the eastern sky. I was too fraught with excitement and tension in equal measure to even consider sleep, so I sat by the fireplace and smoked a succession of pipes. There was little conversation—Holmes had retreated back into his head. He had the ring in his palm, and would look at it occasionally, turning it over, studying the band, and every now and then perusing the strange jet-and-silver sigil.

"We need to get back to Hackney, Watson," he finally said when a noise from the scullery below told us that Mrs. Hudson was up and about, only an hour later than usual.

"Not me, old bean," I replied. "At least not today. I have patients to attend to."

"Very well," Holmes replied. "I shall report any findings on your return this evening."

As luck would have it, I had the busiest day I'd had for

several years, and I was as tired as an old dog after a long walk by the time I returned to Baker Street at seven that evening. My mood was not improved by the sight of Holmes sitting by the fire with a face like thunder.

"It did not go well, Watson," was all he said at the time. "The trail has gone cold."

I only pried the gist of the matter out of him in dribs and drabs over the course of the evening. His visit to Hackney had been fruitless; there was nothing of note to be found in the church or its grounds. No one in the area—of those few who would deign to speak—knew the identity of our dead burglar. To cap it all, Mrs. Green seemed to have taken a turn into early senility, proclaiming that her John was perfectly fine, as she had been hearing his voice telling her so in the night. And as a perfect end to a frustrating day, Holmes' carriage driver had not been as patient as our man from the previous day, and Holmes had been forced into a long walk home in sweltering heat.

"Green saw something," he said, several times during the evening. "It is the only possible explanation. But without a trail—or a body—I have nothing to follow, no facts to digest."

I have seen Holmes frustrated in the past, but rarely had a case vexed him so mightily as this. That first night he took to the violin, sawing away mournfully long into the night. If Mrs. Hudson or myself had our sleep disturbed, we were too experienced in Holmes' moods to broach the subject in the morning.

Until his next case—which thankfully came within the week, Holmes spent long hours in the armchair by the fire studying the ring—the only tangible piece of evidence in our possession. But no amount of examination would force it to yield its secrets. Once the new case caught his attention, I believed that Holmes had put the matter aside, but one evening in October I came upon him at his study table, hunched over the ring once again, examining it with his large glass.

"There's not a single jeweler in the city professes any knowledge of this blasted ring, Watson," he said as I entered. "And no goldsmith knows how, where, or why it was made. I cannot find another representation of the sigil in any book, magical tome or artwork from any civilization in history, and the diamond in the center isn't a diamond at all, although there is no expert in jewels, mineralogy or crystallography who can tell me what it might be. It draws at the mind somehow, a draining sensation that tests me, Watson. It tests me sorely."

That night I managed to persuade him to leave the apartments and take in a show. The operetta seemed to divert his attention readily enough. On returning home he did not mention the ring again, although I noticed in the morning that it was no longer on his desk.

It was near Christmas before the ring and the story behind it came back to mind. Knowing Holmes, I doubt it was ever far from his, but I had pushed it away under the pressure of other concerns and was taken somewhat by surprise at the next turn of events.

7

I was still abed, having spent the previous night at the Officer's Club with too few old friends and too much gin, so I was not best pleased to be woken on a frosty December morning by Holmes banging loudly on my door.

"Get up, old man. We have somewhere to be."

I washed and dressed as quickly as possible, but even so, Holmes was almost beside himself with irritation. I had time to grab two slices of cold toast before he was off and away down the stairs. By the time I reached the street outside, Holmes had already hailed a carriage. We hopped inside, and he took his time in lighting up a cheroot before deigning to explain matters to me—not that his explanation made me any the wiser.

"Lestrade has what he has called 'a right peculiar corpse,' for us to look at, Watson," Holmes said through a fug of smoke.

"And what in blazes does he mean by that?"

"We don't yet have enough facts to form a theory," Holmes said. "Indeed, we only have one fact, but it may prove pertinent. The body was found in Hackney."

I have had occasion to visit the morgue in the Yard numerous times. It never gets any more pleasant. Cold gripped me on entry, a damp chill that ate deep inside and was worse than any night watch I had ever endured in the Afghan foothills. It never seemed to bother Holmes. He strode forward, ignored

Lestrade and the three officers alongside, and started a study of the body on the slab in the center of the room.

He beckoned me over to join him.

"What do you make of this, Watson?" he said.

The body had its back to me, so the first thing I saw was the gaping hole in the skull. It was only on close inspection I saw that it had been made as part of a surgical procedure. The body was cold to the touch, colder even than had it been lying in the morgue for several hours—it had lain in the open for quite some time. Even so, the extensive wounds were clear enough. I stood back, disgusted by the thought that a man in my profession might have performed such a deed.

"Someone has taken his brain—they were dashed careful about it, too. The brain, and most of the spinal column by the looks of it. Who would do a thing like that?"

Holmes' lips were pursed tight.

"Perhaps the identity of the brain's owner might give us a clue."

I walked round the body and stopped when I saw what Holmes was getting at—I knew this man, had last seen him lying, dead—as I had thought—on the floor of his dressing room.

John Green was no longer a missing person.

"So you can confirm it is him, then?" Lestrade said. "Our missing memory-man?"

"It is indeed," Holmes replied. "And he may have been missing these four months and more, but he has only been dead a matter of days by the looks of the body. Where exactly was he found?"

"In 'Ackney Marshes, on the north bank of the Lea, sir," one of the younger officers replied. "A man on his way home from night shift came across him—right sudden, he said—

gave him a terrible shock and …"

"All right, lad," Lestrade butted in. "We don't need chapter and verse. He's dead. That's an end to it."

"On the contrary, Lestrade," Holmes said. "I believe we are merely at the end of the beginning."

Holmes would brook no disagreement—he had to see the scene.

"And quickly too, before half of London has trampled over it."

Five minutes later we were on our way to Hackney once more. At least on this trip we had no worries about our driver leaving us stranded, for Lestrade accompanied us and we traveled in one of the Yard's carriages, but the inclement weather had made the streets treacherous, and going was slow, especially after we left the city center. There was ample time for Lestrade to infuriate Holmes with a serious of questions that as yet could not possibly be answered. It took my friend ten minutes to get exasperated, which was five minutes longer than I had expected.

"So where's the rest of him, then?" was the latest question, and the one that finally caused Holmes to sigh in exasperation.

"All in good time, Lestrade. You only asked me to become involved this morning, remember?"

"I should say you involved yourself several months back, Holmes. Or do I have to remind you about the dead man we found tied in your chair?"

I saw Holmes bristle—that was the moment where the case became a personal matter of pride for him, and I knew then that we would pursue it until the bitter end. At the time, I had no idea how far away that end might be.

The carriage took a more direct route to Hackney Marshes than on our previous trip, so we avoided the almost-derelict area around the old church and found ourselves out on the flatlands to the north, in a winter landscape. Snow had fallen here overnight, and then frozen to a crisp layer that crackled underfoot as we disembarked.

It was immediately apparent where the body had lain — the snow for several yards around was tinged pink, and there was a body-shaped indentation in the soft mud of the riverbank. Holmes had also been right about the police officers — the marks of their boots were apparent across the whole area.

"Whoever did it certainly made no attempt to conceal the body," Holmes remarked dryly, eyeing the open spaces all around us. He set about his customary minute examination of the immediate area despite the bitter cold. Lestrade and I were more circumspect and returned to the carriage, where I partook of a hair-of-the-dog Scotch from his hip flask in return for a smoke. The flask was empty and we were on our second cigarillo before Holmes stepped up into the carriage. His face was pale, with only two small patches of color on his cheeks, and ice crystals had formed in his eyebrows, but Holmes seemed not to notice any physical discomfort when his mind was fully occupied.

"There are no prints apart from police-issue boots, neither coming or going from any direction," he said. "Dash it all to blazes — it is as if he fell out of the sky."

He leaned out and pointed up the hill towards where the old church and graveyard looked out over the plain. "Driver — take us up there. I have a feeling that if we are to find any answers, that is the only place they will be."

The carriage struggled to climb the slope in the snow, and we had to get out and walk some way from the top, so we got a full view of both the church and the street beyond as we walked into the graveyard from the north end.

The street had been covered in an inch of snow, with no sign of footprints anywhere to break the expanse of white. No fires burned in the houses, no smoke rose from any of the chimneys, and there was not even the sound of a bird to break a silence so deep that none of us felt much like speaking.

"If I were you, I'd bring some men out here," Holmes said softly to Lestrade. "I think you have more than one missing person to worry about now."

Lestrade went back to relay a message to the carriage driver, while Holmes and I made a circumnavigation of the church. We trod through crisp snow; there was no indication that anyone but us had been near the building since the snowfall.

Holmes walked towards the church door. I pulled him back.

"We should check on Mrs. Green first," I said. "If she is still here, she might need medical assistance. And in any case, she deserves to know of her husband's fate."

"That is Lestrade's domain, not mine," Holmes said.

"Nevertheless, the lady knows us—it would be best for bad news to come from a familiar face."

I thought Holmes might argue the case, but as I walked towards number 23, I heard his footsteps crackle in the snow behind me.

Mrs. Green was long past the stage of needing my expertise—we found her in her parlor, partially frozen to her armchair. It was clear that she had been dead for several days at least.

"Is it a coincidence, Holmes, she and her husband dead so close to each other?"

Holmes stood up from where he had been studying the body. "I do not believe in coincidences—not in this case," he muttered.

We made a quick search of the house, but found nothing of note that would yield any clues, and no sign that anyone other than Mrs. Green herself had lived there at any time recently—certainly no sign that John Green might have been home in the months since his disappearance. As we left the building and went back out into the road, Lestrade arrived through the graveyard.

"We have another body for you, Inspector," Holmes said. "And she, too, is in a chair, but on this occasion you cannot lay the blame at our door for putting her there."

Lestrade looked up and down the street—it was still as quiet and lacking in activity as when we arrived. "What happened here, Holmes?"

"At a guess? I would say almost everyone simply left—apart from poor Mrs. Green, who waited, as long as she was able, for her husband to come home to her. There may well be others who have suffered a similar fate—this place smells far too much of death for my liking."

Holmes strode off at speed, back towards the church.

"Come on," he called over his shoulder. "There must be something. There is always something."

"Give me a hand here," Holmes said. "It was a bit stiff back in August, and I fear the cold has made it worse."

The church door finally yielded under pressure as the three of us put our shoulders to it, and we almost fell inside when it gave way. It felt strangely warm inside, especially when compared to the chill that had pervaded Mrs. Green's small parlor, but there was no obvious sign of a heat source.

Holmes had us stand back as he studied the floor. He looked disappointed when he turned to motion us forward.

"There are no footprints but mine. No one else has been here these four months past."

We sidled past the tangled heap of broken chairs and pews I had seen from outside the window on our previous visit, and stood in front of the stone altar. The roof immediately above us was open to the elements at this point, but no snow lay on the altar or on the floor around it. Holmes put his hand out, moving it above and around the stone.

"There is a draft here—warmer air coming up from below. I would not have noticed it in the heat of August. Lend me a hand, if you please, Watson."

He pushed at the altar. The old stone grated and squealed—and slid a good inch. A gust of air, even warmer still, blew past us, and with it came a smell I knew only too well—the rotting stink of putrefaction.

"It is a crypt, Holmes," I said. "There is nothing to be found there but more death."

"We shall see about that," he said, and put his weight against the altar again, moving it another inch.

In the end it took all three of us to shift the old stone, but finally we had it slid aside sufficiently far that we could look down on where a flight of timeworn stone steps led deep into the dark.

The rising air smelled—and tasted—rank and foul, but only for a few seconds, and then the assault on our nasal passages seemed to clear as the colder, fresher air from above mixed through it. Holmes took out a handkerchief and put it over his face. He peered down the steps.

"Holmes, don't."

My request fell on deaf ears.

"There is light down there, Watson. And possibly answers."

Before we could stop him, he headed down into the dark. I had no option but to follow. It was only a dozen or so steps down, but oppressive heat grew with each one, and the smell, although dispersing gradually, was still almost enough to make me nauseous. I was trying hard to keep my stomach under control, so I did not notice that Holmes had stopped at the foot of the steps. I almost barged into him, apologized, and then stopped myself, struck immobile and dumb by the sight in front of us.

The room was lit from high overhead—by descending the steps we had moved out from under the foundations of the church and were now somewhere under the graveyard, with thin sunlight coming in through snow-covered grates high above. It showed what we had discovered all too clearly—I almost wished for darkness.

There were six of them—six mutilated and bloody bodies in varying stages of decomposition, lying atop six ancient sarcophagi. Each body, like Green's back in the morgue, had its brain and spinal column surgically removed. There was no sign of the removed organs.

I finally got some degree of control over my faculties and started forward, but Holmes pulled me back.

"Look, Watson, on the floor."

The floor was deep with dust, and covered with marks, but they looked less like footprints, more like the scratching of some huge insect or bird.

"Can you smell it?" Holmes said.

At first I thought he was talking about the putrefaction, and then it came to me, stronger than before: the definite tang of a vinegar-like acid.

"There's more," Holmes said, and directed my gaze to the far end of the crypt. It was gloomier over on that side, but what Holmes wanted me to see was clear enough. There, carved on the wall in bas-relief, and obviously of great antiquity, was the very same sigil that was etched in silver and jet on the ring.

8

Lestrade soon had his hands full trying to control the growing chaos that comes with a multiple murder, and sent us off in no uncertain terms once officers started to arrive on the scene.

"Six more bodies? The Chief would have my guts for gaiters if he knew I'd let you anywhere near them. I'll try to find time to see you in Baker Street later," he said. "But I can't promise you anything—not in a case like this."

We went up into the clear air while police doctors and uniformed constables crowded into the crypt below. Holmes was never the one to stand idly by while others charged ahead, and he lasted less than ten minutes before declaring that he would not countenance staying in Hackney merely to observe the comings and goings of Lestrade's investigation.

"Come, Watson, let us approach this from another direction," he said, and walked away down the deserted street so quickly that I had to break into a trot to catch up with him.

We did not have the luxury of a waiting carriage. We walked, heading south, neither of us speaking for some time. It was only as we moved into busier streets that Holmes made his thinking known to me.

"What do you make of it, Watson? Why would anyone perform such operations? And why in a musty crypt?"

I had indeed been thinking on it.

"I mentioned Far Eastern cults when we first discovered

the ring—these have medicines made from animal parts: bull's pizzles, rhino horn and the like, and there is a great deal of money in the business. Perhaps these procedures are to procure materials that are part of that trade?"

"Perhaps," Holmes said. "But I cannot get my mind off the sigil on the wall. It is important; I feel it—I have known it since I first saw it. Come. Let us see if we can uncover its meaning."

We reached the city center at lunchtime, but if I thought Holmes might allow us some time for victuals, I was to be disappointed. I was acutely aware that I had only eaten two pieces of toast since last night's indulgences, but Holmes was deaf and blind to the needs of the body when a case had hold of him.

Our first stop was to the British Library, not to peruse the shelves, but for Holmes to nudge one of his many contacts to undertake some research on our behalf. A florin changed hands, and Holmes gave a description and details of the old church, the ring and the sigil, and then we were off quickly to another port of call, a bookstore tucked away off Charing Cross Road that I had never before noticed. Holmes, however, seemed well-acquainted with the owner, a thin, balding chap of indeterminate age who again received a florin, and the same descriptions as before.

Our third visit was to a tiny Chinese medicinal store behind Berwick Street—I knew there was an opium den in the cellar below—every doctor in the city knew of that place, and if I knew, Holmes also must know. But that was not the purpose of our visit. Two florins changed hands this time, as Holmes asked to be told news of any trade in brains or spinal columns.

By this time I was becoming rather tired and leg-weary, and more than a bit cold.

"Just one more thing, old chap," Holmes said. "Then we'll see if Mrs. Hudson can rustle up some soup."

The last thing proved to be a stop on the corner most favored by the group of local boys Holmes called, with no little affection, his Baker Street Irregulars. More coins changed hands—ha'pennies and pennies in the main this time, and the boys dispersed quickly, like shadows, all gone into the surrounding streets by the time Holmes returned to my side.

"And now, we wait," he said.

The redoubtable Mrs. Hudson had anticipated our needs with her usual, almost telepathic efficiency, and we lunched on some piping hot potato-and-carrot soup with cheese buns fresh out of the oven. I have rarely had a more welcome meal, and by the time we lit up a smoke and settled down with a cup of tea by the roaring fire, I felt disinclined to venture any further that day.

My resolve not to leave the comfort of the fire was strengthened by a growing darkness outside, and a deadening of all sound of the city that told me fresh snow was falling, and in some quantity too. I finished my smoke and my tea and was drifting into a peaceful reverie when we heard a carriage door slam outside, and then a heavy knock on the door downstairs.

"Wake up, Watson. Mycroft has deigned to leave his lair. It must be important."

I did not know how Holmes knew the identity of the caller; it could be anything from the sound of the carriage, the heft of the knock on the door, or even the speed at which Mrs. Hudson moved to answer. All I know is that he was rarely wrong in such matters, and our landlady showed Mycroft Holmes in a minute later.

I had not seen Holmes' brother for some time, and I was surprised to see him looking gaunt and rather unwell despite the fact that he seemed to have gained several pounds in his already-portly bulk. He sat in the offered armchair, resting himself down in it as if he had just undertaken an inordinate amount of exercise, and dropped the satchel he carried to his feet, letting out a satisfied sigh of contentment.

He waved away my show of concern.

"A touch of lumbago," he said. "The cold weather makes it worse. It's nothing a glass of port won't cure."

I took the hint, went to the cabinet and returned with a bottle and three glasses. I poured Mycroft's first, and he was ready for another before I had sat down. It was only after he was halfway down that one, and had got a cigarette lit in his long ebony holder, that he broached the reason for his visit.

He addressed Holmes directly, which was rare, for he often preferred to use me—at the start of things at least—as a buffer between their mutual animosity on the infrequent occasions when they needed to talk to one another civilly.

"You were there in Hackney this morning when they found the bodies," he began. It wasn't a question, and Holmes didn't reply. "Lestrade thinks he is after a maniac, and much of the city is inclined to agree with him—there are already rumors spreading of a foreign sailor with a grudge. The Yard will have its hands full keeping panic and mayhem off the streets in the coming nights. But that's the Yard's problem. I'm here because Lestrade may be wrong in his conclusion as to the nature of the killer."

Holmes looked up. Mycroft had seized his attention.

"There have been other cases."

That also wasn't a question. I have watched the Holmes brothers indulge in their cat-and-mouse conversations on many occasions and I was expecting something similar here, with Holmes having to work for every scrap of information that Mycroft deigned to provide. For once the older brother seemed too weary for the game, and showed his hand almost immediately.

"In the satchel, if you'd be so kind, Watson?"

I passed the satchel to Holmes—it was indeed heavier than it looked, and we found out why when Holmes opened it. It was full of files—half-a-dozen brown cardboard folders marked with the official crest of the House of Lords.

"They cannot leave my sight," Mycroft said. "I might be tried for treason if anyone found out I have shown them to you, but I know you will not drop this case, and you would find out eventually, so ..."

Holmes had already begun looking through the files. "Rome, Rio de Janeiro, Moscow, Cairo, Philadelphia, Delhi, Jakarta. It is worldwide, then?"

Mycroft nodded. "And all in the last six months, all with the same *modus operandi*—the brains and spinal cords are surgically removed and the bodies left on display like so much meat. Twenty-three bodies at the latest count. Given the widespread nature of the phenomenon, the pattern might never have been noticed ..."

"... if you did not spend most of your time looking for exactly this kind of thing?"

If Holmes was attempting to get a rise out of his brother, it did not work. Mycroft polished off his second port and waved the empty glass in my direction.

"If you please, Watson? Just one more; then I have to be going. There's some trouble brewing in Prussia."

"Isn't there always?" Holmes replied, and got a thin smile in return.

"I cannot leave anything with you," Mycroft said. "But you have the basics already. Given the distances and time involved for traveling between murders, I believe we are looking at multiple assailants—and given the exactness of the surgery, the attention to detail and the similarities in methodology, I can only surmise we are dealing with a conspiracy."

Holmes did not reply to that, but studied the files in front of him, one after the other. I knew he was storing it away to be analyzed later, in case there was something both he and Mycroft had missed on their first pass.

Mycroft was finishing up his port as Holmes tidied up the paperwork and placed it carefully back in the satchel. Mycroft pushed himself, with some difficulty, out of the chair.

"We will stay in close touch on this one?" he said.

Holmes nodded.

"As you say, given the international nature of the thing, we might have need of your contacts."

"And I may even have need of some of yours," Mycroft replied, taking the satchel from Holmes and clutching it to his chest. "Just find me something to work with, Sherlock. We're all operating in the dark at the moment."

It was only after Mycroft left that I realized he had not spoken of the sigil or the ring.

"It may be that he does not consider them important," Holmes replied when I mentioned the fact. "Or it may be that he is still playing some cards close to his chest. In any case, I was not going to mention it if he did not. It may be our only real way to slip between the cracks in this investigation—let us hope so, at least, for there is precious little else to be going on with."

9

Lestrade, as good as his word, did indeed find time to visit us, late in the evening after our supper and just in time to prevent me from heading for my bed.

He looked weary and harassed—seven bodies all at once had, as Mycroft said, garnered a lot of attention very quickly, and Lestrade had the misfortune to be the public face of the Yard on this occasion. It was not a role he relished.

"I am a policeman, not a bleeding newspaper-man," he said when he came in. "Why does everyone think I have all the answers?"

I poured him a stiff drink and he gulped it gratefully before joining us by the fire.

He had little to say beyond what we already knew. They had identified two of the bodies so far, but neither gave any clue as to why they had been killed—one was a lady of letters from Wokingham and the other an office clerk at an insurance broker in the city. Lestrade had men looking for any connection between those two and Mr. Green, the memory-man, but I felt in my gut that he would find none—our quarry was proving too elusive, too intelligent, to have chosen victims with a personal connection.

Like Mycroft before him, Lestrade did not immediately mention the sigil, despite its prominence on the crypt wall, and despite having himself seen the ring, but he was too good a policeman to have missed the implication of it showing up at the scene. He brought it up just as he was leaving.

"I'll leave the business with the ring and the pretty patterns to you, shall I, Holmes?" he said. "I have enough on my plate as it is with the bodies."

Holmes nodded.

"I doubt there is anything for you to find beyond the singular nature of the medical procedures," Holmes said. "Although it may be worthwhile inquiring as to the nature of the minds of those killed. Mr. Green had a brain like a vast library—if you discover that the others were equally gifted, then we might have another fact to add to the small pile we have gathered."

"I shall get right on it," Lestrade said, his tiredness allowing his sarcasm to show as he left.

I left Holmes in the seat by the fire and finally was able to make my weary way to a most welcome bed where, I am glad to say, I slept the sleep of the just through a long, undisturbed night.

Holmes wasn't in the chair in the morning, but any hope I might have had that he himself had partaken of a good night's sleep was dashed when I heard him shout in the hall downstairs.

"Mrs. Hudson—some cake for these hungry boys, if you please?"

I arrived in the sitting room just as Holmes showed two of his street lads inside, making them remove their shoes before allowing them entrance to the parlor in a rare nod to Mrs. Hudson's pride in the carpeting.

The boys were wide-eyed and obviously in awe of both Holmes and the surroundings in which they now found themselves. I knew for a fact that some of these children lived hand-to-mouth on the streets, snatching sleep where they could, and living off what scraps they could find and pennies they could beg. Here, inside a house, they were out of their natural habitat, and it showed. They perched on the edge of chairs much too large for them, and looked like a pair of frightened rabbits ready to flee at the slightest provocation.

Mrs. Hudson's delivery of freshly baked cake helped to keep them still, although did little for the conversation while they coated their lips—and chins—liberally with cream and jam. All too quickly they were ready for more, but Holmes withheld a second helping just out of their reach.

"So you have found something, have you? Something worth another piece of this splendid fancy?"

The boys nodded in unison, their eyes never leaving the plate.

"It were over in that old church on the edge of Russell Square," the bolder of the two spoke up. "St. Columba's, I fink they calls it—it's been empty for years. Right creepy place it is too—we don't go there much in the dark. But there's been stories, see, these three weeks past."

"And we know you likes stories, Mr. Holmes, sir," the other butted in, their confidence growing as their excitement rose.

"So we goes over there and hung around last night, waiting, like. And the boogers came, just after midnight."

"*Who* came?" Holmes asked softly.

"The mad monks," the smaller boy said, his eyes wide. "Ten of them, with long cloaks and 'oods over their heads, singing and chanting and all kinds o' stuff and nonsense."

"There was them lights too, Mr. Holmes, high up inside the old church—green and blue and red and shining—fair hurt my eyes to look at them, so it did."

"And the monks went inside?"

The boys nodded.

"And what then?"

It looked as though the older boy might not reply, until the smaller one dug an elbow, sharp into his ribs.

"We went closer and had a look," he said, barely above a whisper. "Tiny here nearly peed himself, but he's a brave lad and watched my back as I went to the window. And there it were, bold as brass, up on the wall—that thing you showed us on the ring."

Holmes took out the ring and swiveled the jet face forward.

"This? You are sure?"

The boy went pale, and nodded.

"And then what?"

"Then we felt right queer, like summat had got inside our heads and was poking around in there, and we legged it, sharpish like. I'm telling you no lies Mr. Holmes, I ain't going close to that place again, cake or no cake. It ain't natural."

"And it smells too," the younger lad said. "Stinks o' piss and vinegar."

The boys were more than happy to be paid for their information with more cake, although Mrs. Hudson did not share their joy.

"That was for Doctor Watson, after his supper," she said, with the kind of indignation only a landlady of a certain age can muster convincingly as we met her at the foot of the stairs and Holmes handed her the empty plate. Holmes was unmoved.

"Then it has not gone to waste," he replied. "For I am afraid we may not be back for supper this evening, Mrs. Hudson. We have more pressing matters to attend to." He was already on his way to the door, lifting his heavy overcoat and hat from the coat rack. "That is, if you mean to join me, Watson?"

I gave in to the inevitable, took down my own coat and hat, added a scarf to the ensemble for good measure, and joined Holmes out on the pavement.

Holmes was all for heading directly to the church in Russell Square, but this time I was not ready to comply so meekly to his whims.

"I missed my bally breakfast yesterday. I insist on getting some hot food inside us if we're going to be creeping about in this cold again."

He laughed, and gave in to my demands—he was in a better humor after the boys' story than he had been the night before. The merest inkling of a clue had been enough to raise his spirits considerably.

He even kept me amused over a full breakfast in the Quality Chophouse with a tale of his younger days at University he had never before related. It proved to be a most humorous story featuring a Bishop, a prostitute and a policeman that would cause quite a public scandal if the details were ever made public.

We were both in fine spirits as we hailed a cab for Russell Square, but my feelings of well-being lasted only as long as it took the weather to change and sleety drizzle to set in for the duration. I was of half a mind to leave Holmes to it and ask our driver to take me straight back to Baker Street, but if truth be told, the boys' story had me intrigued enough to want to know if there was anything to it.

The carriage eventually dropped us off at the corner of Russell Square after having to take several detours north of

Blackfriars due to impassable roads. The inclement weather had driven most people off the streets, and there was no one else in the vicinity as we approached Saint Columba's church.

I knew the building well—I even remembered it when it had last been in use some ten years past, having attended a Forces funeral that filled the old place with the skirl of pipes and heartfelt hymns. The intervening decade had not served the building well, and it was a sad shadow of its former glory. The only saving grace was that once we pushed open the doors and headed inside we were sheltered from the worst of the sleet—but not all of it, for the roof had partially fallen in on the western side.

Half a dozen pigeons noisily noted our presence as we picked our way through broken timbers and shattered pews. It was obvious as we approached the altar that some attempt had been made at clearing this area. I was about to mention it to Holmes, when I saw that he had stopped, and was staring up at the expanse of empty wall above the lectern.

Someone had been busy with paint—busy and rather hasty, for the strokes had run and streaked in several places, but the image portrayed was clear enough—we had once again come face to face with the radiating rays of the unfathomable sigil.

Holmes immediately started a search of the surrounding area. I stood back, far enough to keep out of his way and to give myself some shelter from the elements, and had a smoke. I have known Holmes to peruse locations for hours on end, lost in his quest for minutiae that might shed light on the task at hand. I was used to waiting, and had prepared myself for more of the same, but on this occasion I did not have to wait long.

"The Irregulars were telling the truth—at least as they saw

it," Holmes said. "There have indeed been many people wearing robes in the vicinity—you can clearly read their movements by the scuff-marks in the dust." He pointed at an area of flooring that looked just like the rest to me. "They mostly congregated around the daubing on the wall, in a tight group. And what's more, there's a lot of those blasted insect-like scratch marks too—the same as the ones we saw in the crypt. Whatever is going on here, it is most definitely linked to the event in Hackney. And we finally have a clue—something I can work with. I found this."

He held up an inch long stub, the remains of a cigarillo that still had a gold band two-thirds of the way down along its length. He sniffed at it and nodded.

"Moroccan," he said. "As I would have surmised from the color and texture—and it is fresh, smoked at the same time as the gathering here, I would wager."

"Does it really get us anywhere, Holmes?" I asked.

He smiled.

"It may get us a long way, Watson. I know of only one supplier of this particular brand in the city. These are expensive—far out of the pocket of your common criminal classes. With luck we may even be able to find the man who bought it."

Holmes put the stub away in an envelope—he kept some at hand at all times for just these occasions—and tucked it in his pocket before continuing.

"There are yet other marks in the dust but they are most perplexing, as there are no indications of its coming or going, as if something just appeared, and then left again as mysteriously as it had come. And as to the nature of whatever ceremony took place, I am as yet at a loss. A cigarillo stub is not much to be going on with—but if the case demands that we must move in small steps, then that is what we shall do."

The drizzly sleet abated somewhat, and it was only then that I noticed the Irregulars had been right about something else.

The odor of vinegar pervaded the whole place.

10

A trip to a tobacconist in the Strand with the cigarillo stub yielded the first clue of any note to turn up in the case—or rather, two clues, for the tobacconist remembered two recent purchasers of the Moroccan cigarillos.

"I only remember as they both asked for them specifically—I hear they are a fine strong smoke, although I never touch them myself—I'm more of a Virginia man—indeed, I have some new leaf just arrived if I can interest you in …"

Holmes cut the man off. "The cigarillos—could you tell me the names of the buyers?"

"I might," the man said, and I recognized the look that came to his eyes only too well. After the inevitable haggling, he gave us the names; it cost Holmes a crown, but he considered it money well spent. I recognized one of them— Sir David Patrick was a surgeon in the higher echelons of that career in the Royal Hospital—I'd never met the man, but had also never heard a bad word said against him. The other name, John Mains, was unfamiliar to me—but not to Holmes.

"He's in shipping," Holmes said. We had been caught in a heavier bout of sleet immediately after leaving the tobacconists in the Strand, and so combined sheltering with lunching in the George over a pint of porter and a splendid pork pie. "Most of his business is done through Glasgow, and comes in from the Southern Hemisphere—timber and spices mainly, although there have been rumors that large quantities of opiates are often among his cargoes, which is how he came to my attention. I believe he maintains a house in town—it should not be too difficult to track him down."

Holmes left me to my pie and went to the bar. More coins passed hands as Holmes went from table to table. I was struck yet again with the ease with which Holmes could drop into conversation with anyone, from the poorest laborer to the richest banker, yet find common ground. It took him less than five minutes in the bar to find someone who knew Mains' address and was willing to divulge it. This time, it only cost him the price of two pints of ale to find out that the man had a place within two streets of the church in Russell Square.

"It seems we have found our man—or one of them, in any case," Holmes said on his return to the table. "Shall we beard him in his den, Watson?"

"And say what, old chap? We have no real evidence with which to attack him—we do not even know whether this thing in the church is not just some mummery—fun and games for rich men with too much money and time on their hands."

"Oh, it is more than that, Watson—I am sure of it. We will know soon enough. But first let us return to Baker Street—I have hopes that my man in the British Library will have come up with something for us by now. We may yet find something we can use to coax Mains to talk to us."

As fate would have it, Holmes' hopes were justified. On our return to Baker Street, we found an envelope on the coat-rack in the hallway, addressed to Holmes in a neat but cramped hand. It contained three sheaves of paper, with writing on both sides.

We went upstairs, and I had a smoke while Holmes perused the letter. By the time Mrs. Hudson brought us a pot of tea, he was done. He handed it to me.

"Well, it is certainly *something*, Watson," he said. "But I am not sure it is pertinent to our case today."

It took me several seconds to become accustomed to the man's writing style, it being both cramped and rather too flowery in language for my taste, but that was soon forgotten. It quickly became clear that Holmes' man in the Library had indeed uncovered the history of the sigil—a long and involved one at that, albeit one cloaked in secrecy. His notes told of a sky-god cult that dated back into pre-Roman antiquity, being particularly prevalent in the area now known as the Scottish Borders, and having been added by the Romans themselves to the long list of cults and myths incorporated into the soldiers' worship along Hadrian's Wall.

The cult was almost completely forgotten in the modern era, and the only mention in antiquity was by a monk in Lindisfarne in the eighth century. He described it as an unspeakable blasphemy that must not be mentioned. The other fact—if it could be classified as such—was that the sigil signified the above and the below—the stars and the earth, waiting for the sky-gods who would return one day to fulfill a promise of leading us to some vague, better, future.

It was all rather wishy-washy, to my mind.

"I may have been right, Holmes," I said. "It all sounds like a case of rich men with too much time on their hands playing silly sods—wasn't there a gathering of Mithras worshippers in the Temple a few years back? And wasn't that just an excuse for them to imbibe too much liquor and fondle some ladies of rather loose morals?"

Holmes sighed.

"You may indeed be correct in your assumption, Watson. I cannot yet see the connection between this frippery and the murders. But there is one. I would stake my reputation on it."

Holmes had managed to stay still for the time it took to smoke a pipe, but as soon as I handed the papers back to him, he jumped to his feet.

"Bearding the Scottish lion in his den it is, then. Come, Watson; it is time to find out if our Mr. Mains is involved in anything more than injudicious drinking and wenching."

I had Holmes wait long enough for me to fetch my service revolver. When he saw that I was armed, he lifted his stout cane from the rack in the hallway, and slapped the heavy head in the palm of his hand.

"Let us see if we can stir up some trouble," he said, and then smiled. "I'm sure Lestrade will like that."

The Mains residence was a large detached dwelling in a row of similar buildings to the north of Russell Square—the sort of area stockbrokers and insurance men flee back to after their days in the city, a small oasis of relative calm in the teeming urban bustle. I have heard rumors that local policemen can get paid under the table for putting in extra patrols in this vicinity. Seeing this particular street, I could quite believe it— we weren't far from some rather rough areas, but this avenue was even quieter than some of the leafy suburbs further out of town. Our carriage was the only traffic.

After alighting, we went though an open gate and along a short driveway that led up to an imposing front door. Holmes rapped, using a large cast-iron knocker that showed the Lion Rampant crest of Scotland—another clue that we might be in the right place after all.

A butler who looked as if he would be more at home

watching the door in a Glasgow bar showed us inside. He may have been a mute, for he didn't speak a word, and did not ask our names. When I looked over at Holmes, he raised an eyebrow and smiled.

"It seems we are expected, Watson. The old-boy network has been at work; I suspect the tobacconist has several more coins in his pocket."

The silent butler led us into a very grand library, opulently built in mahogany and leather, containing shelf after shelf of fine tomes that looked as if they had never been touched, never mind read. The whole room had that new, clean feeling you would never encounter in an old library, and I had a feeling it had been put together sometime in the last year or so at the earliest.

Mains stood by an imposing marble fireplace—a small, stocky man with very bushy black eyebrows and a mop of gray hair that he tried, unsuccessfully, to keep in check with lashings of oil that I smelled clear across the room. He was dressed for dinner, and had a brandy snifter in one hand and a cigarillo in the other—Moroccan, with a gold band.

"Whatever you have to say, make it quick," he said, addressing Holmes directly. "I have business to attend to in half an hour."

"Good," Holmes said, dropping into a chair and setting about lighting up a smoke. "Then shall we talk about Hackney? I'm sure Lestrade of the Yard will be particularly pleased to hear about your meetings in St. Columba's church, and the painted sigil on the wall—the same sigil that overlooks six dead bodies in another church on the edge of the marshes."

The small Scotsman went pale, and took a deep gulp of his brandy before he was composed enough to reply.

"I can assure you, sir, there is nothing untoward going on in St. Columba's—nothing that would concern the great Sherlock Holmes. And as for Hackney—I have no idea what you are blathering about. If you are accusing me of involvement in some nefarious activity, I must ask you to leave immediately."

Holmes had his smoke going to his satisfaction, and blew a series of concentric smoke rings in the man's direction.

"In that case, you would not mind inviting us to one of your meetings? I am available tonight, as it happens."

"Out of the question," Mains replied. "I cannot change my plans for the evening at your whim, sir."

"I think you'll find that you can," Holmes said quietly. "I believe you know my brother, Mycroft?" The Scotsman went pale again, and sucked hard on his cigar as Holmes continued. "Mycroft expects you to offer me every courtesy in any request I might make of you in regard to your meetings."

I knew that was an outright lie—but the Scotsman didn't know that. He looked ready to argue, but Mycroft's name carries significant weight in the corridors of power and the highest echelons of the business world, and it was indeed enough in this case for the Scotsman to acquiesce to Holmes' request. He did not, however, have to be pleased about it, and it showed.

"Very well, then," he said, tossing the remains of his brandy into the fire where it flared and sparked. "It so happens that my business and yours now coincide this evening. We have a meeting scheduled, and I am sure you will find it most educational. Give me ten minutes to change; it can get dashed filthy in the church. The others will be arriving at eight. I can assure you, it's all above board—and I am hopeful I might even be able to convince a rational man like yourself to join our cause. But you're right—first you must see for yourself."

I saw something in the man's glance—an almost boyish desire for us to believe him. He looked less like a murderer than any man I have ever seen.

I commented on it to Holmes when we were left alone in the library.

"I saw it too, Watson. Either he is a very good liar, or he has been deceived. Either way, as he has said, we will only know when we see it for ourselves. Keep a hand on your pistol—I suspect things might be starting to move more swiftly."

The night had grown bitterly cold, and we had scarcely gone ten yards from the front door when I started to regret leaving the comfort and warmth of the library.

Mains seemed oblivious to the weather and had turned most eager to tell us all about his meetings—all pretense at secrecy flown now that the decision had been made that we should be allowed to know his business.

"You must agree, Mr. Holmes, that the world has seen too much of war in this past century?" he said.

"I would be a fool to disagree," Holmes replied. "And Doctor Watson here has firsthand experience of much of it."

"And I pray I never have to see any more," I added.

Mains grew animated, a man expounding on a subject that had caught his passion.

"Then what if I told you there was a way—a quick way—to bring about world peace? What if I told you we could be instrumental in ushering in a brave new world with no conflict—a new age of scientific enlightenment?"

"I would say you have had rather too much of your own

brandy," Holmes replied. "Human nature being what it is, and given the state of the world as it is today, I find that particular outcome to be unlikely in the extreme."

"But it is something that would be worth the effort, is it not?"

"That depends on the cost," Holmes replied. "And no amount of verbal fencing out here in the snow will get us anywhere. You are saying that you have a noble reason for your nighttime excursions in the church?"

"Noble? In the main, yes, although without wars, trade could flow more freely and I would also be better off. You see, Mr. Holmes, I am a practical man at heart, not given to flights of fancy—not unless I have seen for myself that the future can be made real, for all of us."

By now I had the man pegged as a zealot. I've met many fanatics in my time, and never found one that could be trusted as far as I could throw him. However, he might possess a clue that would lead us to solving the Hackney crime, so I kept my peace and decided to reserve judgement until we saw what he had to offer. Holmes seemed inclined to do the same, and kept silent as we turned into Russell Square and made once more for the old church.

A huddle of well-dressed men stood just inside the church doorway, and they were, to a man, surprised, if not shocked, to see Holmes and me; our presence started some heated discussion between Mains and the others which took place at the far end of the nave. Holmes seemed to be enjoying himself.

"If nothing else comes out of tonight, Watson, at least we will have had some entertainment."

"It would seem so," I replied. "We have arrived at the

dressing-up-in-silly-costumes part."

Mains seemed to have persuaded the rest of the group that we were not in any way a threat to their activities; they were all already donning long hooded robes. The boys had been right—the robes did indeed make them look like "mad monks."

None of them so much as looked at us as they moved silently to stand in front of the painted sigil. Mains was last to put on a robe, and he came over to where we stood before joining the others.

"There is no trickery here," he said. "No illusion. All that you will see and hear is real. As real as you or I."

And with that cryptic remark, he left us at the back of the church and joined the rest of the group under the painted sigil.

The event started with some atonal chanting that grated on the ears and made me recall some of the acts I had seen in the music hall. It was also rather comical, and I started to think we were on the wrong track after all—it did indeed seem like nothing more than rich men playing silly sods.

Thankfully, the chanting did not last long. Mains moved to the front and raised his arms.

I do not rightly know what I expected, but I was surprised by the dancing aura of lights that rapidly filled the church and cast capering shadows all around us. The lights seemed to come from everywhere, yet nowhere. They were accompanied by a distant hum that grated and caused my teeth to ache. I smelled the sudden tang of vinegar in my nostrils.

The light and color coalesced and thickened, hanging in a flattened oval about the size and shape of a large serving platter in the air between Mains and the sigil. I looked closely but saw no sign of any strings, no indication that any trickery was involved. If an illusion, it was a dashed good one, worthy of any stage.

The surface of the oval dulled to a flat gray and an image gradually formed—a head appeared, out of focus at first, and then sharpening to clarity as a voice spoke, loud and echoing through the church as loud as any vicar's sermon.

"Welcome to your new beginning."

I hardly heard the words—I knew the speaker, and knew I was looking at something impossible, for the man was dead—I had seen his body in the morgue. And yet it was the face of John Green that looked out over the church from within the image, and he smiled as he spoke.

I do believe I might have stepped forward and stopped proceedings then and there, disgusted that this mummery saw fit to desecrate the image of the dead in so blatant a fashion, but Holmes put a hand on my arm, and a finger to his lips.

"Not yet," he mouthed silently.

We watched as Green—or his disembodied head, at least—spoke to the rapt congregation in the church.

"I come to you tonight from the farthest reaches of our planetary system—a place so dark, so remote our scientists do not yet know of its existence. And yet it is here, on Yuggoth, where mankind's ultimate future may yet be born. I have already shared with you details of some of the benefits—and you, and our brethren across the globe, know only too well that the ones I serve are real, and here to help us at this crucial stage of our development. Our task now is to persuade our leaders of the right of our cause."

It struck me to be a singularly uninspiring call to action—there was nothing there to get the old blood pumping, as if it had been written by someone with no sense of what might appeal to a man's soul.

I turned to Holmes, intending to remark on the banality of it all, but he wasn't paying attention to anything on the floor of the church. His gaze was fixed high in the broken rafters above. I tried to peer through the gloom to ascertain what had caught his attention, but saw nothing save a deeper patch of blackness in the shadows.

The congregation still had their full gaze on Green's face.

"The time is coming—and soon, when we shall make the world take notice. Be prepared my friends. We will meet soon, in a better world."

The image faded, the oval shape fell apart into so much light and shadow, and Mains lowered his arms. It seemed the brief show was over.

Again I turned to Holmes to look for his opinion of what had happened, but he was no longer at my side. I looked up to see him picking his way across what was left of the roof, using his cane as a support. And he wasn't alone—he was closing in on the deeper shadow I had noted, but before he got within three yards of it, it moved and spread, like a crow opening its wings. The tang of vinegar got stronger still. There was a brief commotion in the rafters, a flurry and rattle, and then there was just Holmes up there, looking down at us with a puzzled look on his face. He swung himself down and landed, light as a cat, at my side.

"Yet again he was too fast for me—but I am getting his measure, Watson. I shall have him the next time."

The crowd dispersed silently, leaving only Mains alongside

us. He shucked off the robe and smiled.

"Well, gentlemen? What did you think? Did I not tell you there was no wrong-doing to find here?"

"On the contrary," Holmes said softly. "I see the worst kind of wrongdoing of all—I see treachery, possibly even treason."

Mains could not have looked more shocked had he been struck.

"We are working for a better future for all …"

"No," Holmes said, interrupting. "I believe you have been duped by a greater mind than yours. There is no future waiting for you on your current path—only death and misery."

Mains mustered up some bravado. "I have been promised …"

Holmes interrupted again. "And similar promises, I imagine, were made to poor John Green."

"I do not know that name," Mains replied.

"No. But you do know the face. Tell me, Mr. Mains, who is that man who conveys the messages to you?"

The Scotsman shrugged. "We do not know. He appeared to me in my country house several months ago and we began our mission there. All I know is that I trust him implicitly—he is an explorer, a hero, the first of many."

"And the last of a few," Holmes said sadly. "What if we were to take you to Scotland Yard, right now, and show you his body? He has been lying there for some time now, and was certainly not talking to you from some mythical planet tonight, for he is most assuredly dead."

Mains shook his head. "That is not possible."

"Nevertheless, it is the truth," I replied. "If you do not trust Holmes, trust me, as a medical man."

Mains looked back and forth from Holmes to me. "No. I will not have it. This is one of Mycroft's schemes, isn't it? He is trying to stop the future. But it cannot be fought. It is coming, whether the old guard likes it or not."

With that, he turned on his heel and left. I expected Holmes to follow, but he was once again looking up into the rafters, lost in thought.

"Should we go after him?" I asked,

Holmes took his time in replying.

"No—I think he believes what he is saying, more is the pity. Loath as I am to admit it, we must inform Mycroft of what has transpired here—and find out what he has not told us."

11

It was past ten o'clock when we arrived at the Diogenes Club. We were kept waiting, compelled to silence as ever is the case in that establishment. We stood in the reception area for more than twenty minutes before we were shown through to the back room that doubled as Mycroft's office when he was not in Whitehall.

"And you saw this ... apparition?" Mycroft said incredulously as I related our story. Holmes had left the job to me, knowing that Mycroft would not believe me capable of subterfuge in this matter.

"It was no apparition," I replied. "It was some kind of projection, the like of which I have never before seen. But it did not have the feel of anything supernatural—it felt, and looked, mechanical—a piece of advanced engineering was my guess."

Mycroft poured me a glass—a second glass—of his best sherry. It was obvious the tale had given him pause for thought, and he sighed deeply as he sat back in his chair. "And Mains is at the center of this ... conspiracy? You are sure of it?"

"He told us himself that he was the instigator, after an encounter with—whatever it was—in his Scottish home."

Mycroft turned to Holmes.

"Theories?"

"Several," Holmes said curtly. "But not enough facts as yet. You should have told me you knew about the sigil. It might have saved time."

"And you should have told me you had the ring," Mycroft said. "Let us not quarrel—not tonight. There is work to be done."

"The defense of the realm is your domain, not mine," Holmes said, and stood as if to leave.

"And murder is yours," Mycroft said softly. "I fear there will be many more if you do not help me. Sit down. Let me tell you what I know. And what I surmise. Just let me get something started first."

He left us alone—Holmes raised an eyebrow.

"It seems we are once again enlisted for Queen and Country, old chap," he said.

"If it means them adding a few pounds to my service pension, I'm all for it," I replied.

We were both smiling when Mycroft returned, which puzzled him, and made us smile all the more.

"Behave yourselves," he said. "This is important."

Holmes burst out laughing.

"Then tell us, brother. Break the habit of a lifetime and tell me a secret."

Mycroft poured us another sherry before sitting.

"It does not leave this room," he said, and then settled back, half-closed his eyes, and began.

"I knew about the murders—the mutilations, before the thing in Hackney. And at first I did not make the connection with the Sigil—you see, I have also known about Mains' little gatherings, but presumed they were merely bored rich men looking for some rough-edged entertainment. Just last night I discovered these gatherings are rather more commonplace than I knew—there are groups in Bristol, Bath, Edinburgh, Glasgow, and York, alongside at least four others in

London—and those are the ones I know of. I have made inquiries with my international counterparts to see how far the web has grown, but that will take some time. I believe I will hear that this is worldwide; it is big, and it is something we should all fear."

Holmes nodded.

"For once we agree, brother. But it is not the sect of the sigil itself we need to worry about—they are being led, like so many sheep. It is the shepherds we need to find—or rather, as is most likely in my opinion, the wolves in the fold. There is a genius behind all of this we have not yet been allowed to see—just a glimpse here and there, a hint as to the full extent of their plans."

"And how do we find this elusive figure?"

"He started with Mains—and so should we," Holmes said. "The man has a story to tell we haven't heard yet. If Watson and I go after that, I trust you will deal with the rest of the affair?"

"The matter is already in hand," Mycroft said. "All such meetings are now illegal, by act of Parliament, and by command of her Majesty. Any participants will be tried for treason, found guilty, and given a long drop on a short rope. I have men watching all the places I mentioned earlier—we should have everyone in custody within the week."

"Which is all well and good—but without the ringleader, it will all just start again."

"So you will help?" Mycroft said.

"I will catch our murderer," Holmes replied. "You can save the world."

Once again we made our way to Russell Square, hoping to talk to Mains and get the tale of his first encounter with the speaking image—but on this occasion we were to be disappointed.

The town house lay quiet and dark, with no sign of life, no light in any window. The gate in the driveway was now securely locked against visitors.

"It seems our quarry has already fled," Holmes said, and began climbing the tall iron framework. "Let us see if he has left us anything to be going on with."

He turned at the top and saw I hadn't yet followed. He laughed.

"It is just a small bit of burglary, Watson. We are on Her Majesty's Service, remember? Mycroft will not allow us to be jailed for doing the Queen's business."

I am afraid I am not as agile as my good friend, and there was much huffing and puffing before I dropped myself down beside him on the house side of the gate. Despite the noise I had made, the house still sat quiet and still.

Holmes ignored the front door and led me through some tugging and tearing foliage to the back, where a kitchen door looked out over a long expanse of well-maintained lawn. Holmes tried the handle on the off chance it had been left open, and then, when that didn't work, laid his shoulder, hard, against the door above the lock. It gave with a crack, as loud as a gunshot in the night, and swung open. If anyone was at home, the alarm would be sounded any moment now.

We stood in silence for ten seconds. No one shouted, nothing moved.

The door opened directly into an old kitchen area with butler's sinks, copper pans and huge butcher's blocks, little more than dark shadows in the unlit room. Despite the gloom, Holmes seemed to know where he was headed. He led me through to an even darker corridor beyond that was lined in huge oak panels; the black glass eyes of long dead animals followed our passage from high mounts. I was not surprised after a few more seconds to find ourselves at the tall door to the library in which we had met Mains earlier.

Holmes pushed the door open. The room lay in total darkness and silence. Holmes did not hesitate; he lit the lamps on either side of the fireplace, and started to go through the paperwork on Mains' desk. As he was doing so, I made a study of the books—as I expected from our first visit, few of the volumes showed any signs of having been read—a rich man's library, bought for show and containing nothing of any pertinence to our investigation. I turned to tell Holmes, and saw that he was lost in reading from a batch of letters.

"Mycroft was right—it is worldwide. Brazil, Italy," he said, dropping a page for emphasis with each country. "India, Japan, Egypt. Mr. Mains has been busy. But here is what I was looking for."

He showed me a note—it was an invoice from a Scottish butcher for a large quantity of meat.

"Why this, Holmes?"

Holmes tapped the top of the page.

"This is his address in Scotland, Watson—where this thing began, and where we must go to find out where it ends."

I did not have time to reply. As I was passing the note back to Holmes a thud as of someone heavy moving around came from the room directly above us. Holmes and I moved at the same time, each of us putting out a lamp, and although I was not aware of doing so, I realized I now had my pistol in my hand, raised and aimed at the door.

A noise came again above us, this time sounding almost as if someone had fallen out of bed. I smelled a now recognizable hint of vinegar.

Holmes moved away from me, and I saw his silhouette cross against the dim light coming through the window. I followed, my eyes starting to adjust to the gloom as we reached the door, Holmes already heading swiftly and quietly towards the main staircase.

The smell was stronger here, almost burning in my nasal passages. The thudding was repeated, twice, from a bedroom to the right at the top of the stairs. Before I could recommend caution, Holmes ran up the remaining steps with no heed for the noise and burst in the bedroom, his cane raised. I heard him yell, in pain or surprise I knew not. There was a scuffle, as of a fistfight, but it lasted only a second before I heard the crash of breaking glass.

I arrived at the doorway to see Holmes on the floor, the tall bedroom window thrust open to the elements—and a blacker shadow, barely visible, moving off high above the rooftops, flying into the night.

12

It took Holmes several seconds to recover his composure.

"Are you hurt?" I asked.

"Only my pride," he said. "And that can soon be mended."

I helped him to stand. I looked for his cane to pass it to him—it lay on the floor, snapped in two pieces.

"The blighter is dashed strong," Holmes said, as he stood, somewhat groggy, leaning on my shoulder. "I hit him hard, Watson, as hard as I have ever hit anyone. It felt like hitting a wall and as you can see, I need a new Malacca. But there's more—after he returned my blow, and as I was falling, I grabbed out at something, something soft, almost pulpy. I believe I have done him some damage in return for the loss of my dignity."

I lit a bedside lamp—if anyone were going to note our trespassing, they would surely have done so by now—and studied what Holmes had grasped in his left hand. I couldn't for the life of me make sense of what I was looking at. It seemed to be a piece of black shell, shot through with the rainbow colors often seen on rocky shores. And like a shell that had been cracked by a gull, its concave cavity held a wedge of yellow meat, oozing a pale gray fluid that stank of acrid vinegar.

"What in blazes do we have here, Holmes?"

"Another mystery," Holmes replied. "And one we must go to Scotland to solve I'm afraid. But let us first return to Baker Street. I must examine this more closely."

It was in the wee hours of the morning by the time we arrived back in Baker Street, but Holmes showed no sign of tiredness, despite having a bruise the size of a small egg on his temple.

Mrs. Hudson roused herself from bed just long enough to brew us some coffee and provide ham sandwiches and a splendid cold meat pie, and then returned to her quarters mumbling imprecations against unpredictable lodgers, leaving Holmes and me at his study table examining the mysterious substance.

On closer examination, the piece of shell seemed more like that of a crab than any insect, and the inside curve had a most attractive mother-of-pearl sheen to it. The yellowish meat, however, was unclassifiable; it certainly wasn't edible, being slimy and emitting an odor of vinegar so strong I had to keep my head away from immediately above it. Although it was most definitely organic, close examination of the cell structure showed it was closer to plant than animal, with a rigid cell wall that might have been some kind of cellulose but resisted any examination by the admittedly crude equipment at our immediate disposal. There were also mycelia-like strands in a tangled web threaded through the flesh, as if it were infected by—or indeed partly composed of—some form of fungal growth.

One thing both Holmes and I agreed on—it was not anything remotely human.

"And you say it flew?" Holmes asked as we retired to the fireplace for a smoke.

I nodded, remembering my last glimpse of the shadow.

"It might have had wings—or it might have been some kind of balloon or kite—it was too dark to make out any detail."

Holmes went quiet.

"This may be yet more mummery to throw us off the scent," he said. "For the life of me I cannot equate what we have here with the man who assaulted me."

"If it even was a man?" I replied.

Holmes guffawed.

"Come, Watson. If not a man, then what? His actions so far in following and observing us have been all too human, and I can tell you that he punched like a boxer, albeit one with iron in his gloves. No—I must think on this."

We smoked in silence for some time, Holmes growing increasingly still until he was once more in that trancelike state of concentration I was coming to know so well. He did not even twitch when I rose to pour myself two fingers of Scotch.

At some point I grew tired and, before I could act on the feeling, fell asleep in my chair. When I woke to the thin light of morning peering through the curtains, Holmes still sat opposite, puffing on his favorite meerschaum.

"We have had word from Mycroft," he said. "They have rounded up Mains' collaborators from last night, but the man himself slipped the net. It appears he has taken fright—and I believe I know where he will go to ground. What say you, Watson—will you accompany me to Scotland?"

I stood and stretched the kinks out of my poor back.

"Just give me time for a wash and shave. And some breakfast—please?"

Holmes laughed.

"I shall see us on the afternoon train from Euston. Take your time, old chap," he said.

I was not particularly impressed with the emphasis he put on the word 'old'.

The train going north was a quiet one, it being too close to Christmas for the tourist trade, and the weather inclement enough to discourage the casual traveler. We had a carriage to ourselves the whole way and were able to smoke without inconveniencing anyone and to chat without having to worry about being overheard.

Holmes indulged me by doing his thinking aloud, using me as a sounding board for his ideas.

"What we must ask ourselves, Watson, is who has the most to gain from this ... conspiracy, for want of a better word—and who has the skill, and the will, for what is obviously an undertaking on a grand—and grandiose—scale. Each part of that question requires close scrutiny, and unlocking any one part might bring us closer to the truth of the whole. What we can say with some degree of certainty is that Mains, and indeed the whole of the sect of the sigil, have been mere pawns in a larger game. Mycroft may well round them all up and have them disappear from polite society— but the main player remains very much on the board, and very much hidden behind the defenses he has built for himself."

"To continue with the metaphor," I replied. "Are we approaching the end-game?"

Holmes laughed.

"I fear we may still be at the stage of positioning our pieces," he replied. "And I am as yet unsure whether I myself am the white king, or merely another pawn. And as for our opponent—he has shown no scruples about sacrificing pieces when they are no further use to him.

"But it is the advanced machinery that worries me most, Watson. That, and the use they have made of poor Green's face. The manner in which that was accomplished has me completely stumped—it is beyond the ken of what I understand to be the current state of modern science. It may be that we are dealing with an extreme event—a scientist who has made a giant stride forward in scientific thinking independent of all others in his field. And if that is the case—what else might we have to face in our quest for justice?"

"And what of the shell-like material? What are we to make of that?"

Holmes shook his head.

"I do not know, as yet. But it may be merely subterfuge and camouflage. This case began with deception on my part—it may be that our adversary is equally, if not indeed more, adept in that art himself. Facts, Watson—that is all the rational mind can afford to deal in. We need more facts."

"All I have is conjecture," I replied, giving voice to something I had been worrying over. "But what if there is no subterfuge? What if the voice in the image is what it says it is—an emissary from another world, come to help us bring an end to war?"

"By using a dead man's face?" Holmes scoffed. "No, Watson. I cannot be persuaded of the veracity of the most complicated, least obvious solution—not yet in any case, but for the sake of your instincts, I promise not to dismiss it out of hand."

Our journey became somewhat protracted north of Crewe as the weather drew in, and we made slow progress through ever-strengthening winds and steadily building snowdrifts.

The conductor passed through the train and poked his head into our carriage on the way past.

"Jist a wee bit o' snaw," he said in a broad Scots accent.

"Nothing to worry about, gents. We'll be in Carlisle for supper—you'll see."

The train finally came to a grinding halt somewhere to the south of Oxenholme. Icy snow rattled like gunfire against the windows as the light faded and the evening drew on with no seeming prospect of any forward movement.

The conductor poked his head around the door again.

"Should nae be long now, gents," he said, but half an hour later we were still at a standstill. At least the dining carriage stayed open, and we were able to have a supper, albeit one of rather poor quality, which led me to imbibe more ale and Scotch than I perhaps should have. So it was that when nine o' clock came round and there was still no sign of any progress towards Carlisle, I allowed my head to drop, and fell into a doze that quickly turned to sleep.

I was rudely awoken sometime later in a darkened carriage with Holmes bending over me. He had a large syringe in his hand. Even in my slightly befuddled state, I knew this was not a good sign.

"Holmes. You promised me ..."

He smiled thinly.

"This is not for me," he said, at the same time as I heard a loud thud overhead. "We have company."

The thudding came again, louder this time. I followed Holmes out into the corridor, just as the conductor came from the front of the train.

"Nothing to worry about, gents. We have a wee coo on the roof—not so rare as you'd imagine round these parts."

The thudding came again, four quick beats.

"It's a dashed dainty cow," I said. Holmes was already at the carriage door. He pushed it open, letting the wind and snow in, and causing the conductor to sputter and curse in outrage. Holmes wasn't listening. He had already swung himself, one-handed, up onto the slim ledge on top of the doorframe and then outward in one smooth movement onto the carriage roof.

I did my best to follow.

Lashing snow immediately stung my cheeks and threatened to blind me; a gusty wind tugged at my clothes, trying to dash me backward as I pulled myself up. Despite the snow, I saw Holmes clearly enough. He faced an adversary shorter than himself but stocky, broad across both hips and shoulders. Both were mere silhouettes against the darkness of the night, and Holmes' cry of triumph as he raised the syringe came only faintly in the howling wind. His opponent seemed to shudder and quail, and the resulting shriek was louder even than the gale. Holmes made a grab forward, but the other man was still too fast, slipping out of reach to Holmes' left and then leaping—a prodigious jump of some fifteen feet or more—from the roof. The last I saw of him was as a shadow heading over the top of a drift as tall as the train itself; then there was only the snow and wind.

Holmes dashed past me and swung himself in one seemingly effortless movement back into the carriage. I followed rather more sedately, and by the time I got back inside Holmes was remonstrating with the conductor.

"For pity's sake man, I'm only asking for a lantern—not the Crown Jewels."

"I can nae let anyone off the train …" the man started.

"I've already *been* off the bloody train," Holmes said, almost shouting in his face.

The man tried to stand up to Holmes, but there are few men who could look Holmes in the eye when his dander is up. He still, however, would not give in to Holmes' request for a lamp. Holmes turned in disgust and headed off down the train as I did my best to keep up with him.

It took five minutes for us to find a lamp—there were several in the guards' van at the rear. The two gentlemen sitting there were only too happy for us to take what we wanted, although they showed no sign of rising from their seats by a stove to help us.

By the time we got back outside it was too late—I suspect it was too late even when I had my last sight of the shadow going over the top of the snowdrift.

We ventured out into the blizzard and found the tracks easily enough; they were not footprints, but strange, triangular markings, like those a lizard or a large bird might make, and they only went as far as the top of the drift. There they stopped, as if our visitor had vanished into thin air or, as I was coming to fear was the case, had once again taken flight.

13

Sleep was to prove elusive for the remainder of a long, storm-swept night. The train rocked from side to side in the wind, and I started at every thud, expecting our visitor to make a return.

As I gave in to the inevitable and lit up a smoke, Holmes finally showed me the syringe he'd been holding in his lap since his earlier exploits. Half of the fluid within was gone, and the remainder moved sluggishly when I tipped it from side to side.

"Be careful with that, Watson—it's caustic stuff."

I passed the syringe back to him.

"It's not a narcotic, then?" I asked.

Holmes smiled—somewhat wistfully, I thought.

"Not even close, Watson. I surmised that if our opponent was so fond of the acidic, given that it is what we have smelled at each encounter, then maybe some alkali might give him pause for thought—a potassium hydroxide solution seems to have done the trick."

"Did you get a good look at him?"

Holmes went quiet.

"He was enfolded in what appeared to be a leather cloak," Holmes said. "And I believe he wore a mask of some kind of rubber, for it melted and ran when I squeezed the syringe at him—but no, to answer your question, I did not get a close look. I did strike the crucial blow this time, so we could be said to be ahead in the game at this point. And he will pause before testing our defenses again."

We sat there smoking all night, but there was no more thudding overheard, either from leather-clad assailants or from stray bovines. Finally, just as the sun was coming up, the train stirred into life and began to inch forward. A weary cheer rang out along the carriages, followed by a louder one when the conductor came through announcing that the railway would be paying for breakfasts for all.

Breakfast proved a great deal more pleasant than supper and we were fortified with toast, marmalade, bacon and eggs before we finally arrived in Carlisle some twelve hours late. We were, however, fortunate enough to catch an almost immediate connection for Hawick on the Border Union Railway, and we arrived in the market town mid-morning, intending to hire a carriage to take us the last twelve miles to the address we had for Mains.

Once again the weather defeated us. We tried three different carriage drivers and all three turned us away.

"There'll be nowt moving beyond the town boundary at all today," was the general opinion. "And maybe not tomorrow either."

We walked as far as the river that bounded the eastern edge of town, by which time the snow came up almost to our knees—walking twelve miles was not at all possible, especially given that the wind was biting cold, and more snow could arrive at any moment. After our delayed journey to Carlisle, Holmes was champing at the bit to reach our ultimate destination, but even he could see that it would be senseless to try in the conditions.

We took rooms at the Queen's Head, a quite delightful example of a Scottish country inn, and decided we would take our chances with the weather on the morrow.

Our enforced incarceration did mean that I was finally able to grab several hours of restful sleep. I had imagined that Holmes might do the same, but when I rose, refreshed, in mid-afternoon, I found him sitting in the main bar at a table of local chaps, deep in conversation.

The mood seemed cheerful, doubly so when I stood a round for the table.

"I was telling these chaps that we had the pleasure of Mr. Mains' company in London, Watson," Holmes said as I sat. I grunted something non-committal, hoping to gauge the general mood before embarking on conversation. I am glad that I did so, for it quickly became apparent that Mains was a man of some influence in the area, and also seemed to be genuinely liked by all who had met him.

"The new mill has kept many here in work this past year," one man said. "Mr. Mains didn't have to do that—even after the old mill fell into disuse, he had plenty of money to go off and do whatever he liked with it. A smart man like him, he could live anywhere in the world he wanted to."

"And I hear he's planning on starting the old mill up and running again," a younger man said. "There's been folk in and out of there these past few months."

"Queer folk, foreigners and the like, is what I heard," an elderly gent piped up.

"You don't hear anything that don't come out yer arse," another elderly gent said—and so the conversation went, ebbing and flowing around the table, with Holmes doing little more than prodding and leading in the directions he was most interested in.

I spotted that Holmes openly wore the large ring, the lion rampant facing forward. But if any of the men present took any note of it, none said so, even after Holmes swiveled the face around to show the jet-and-silver sigil and left it that way for a good twenty minutes.

One by one our drinking companions dispersed, heading home where wives and sweethearts would be waiting, until finally Holmes and I were left alone at the table. The barman informed us that there was rabbit pie and mash available, so we decided to remain at the table for supper, and while waiting for the food, I was able to catch up with what Holmes had learned.

"The more I hear about our Mr. Mains, the more I am inclined to think that he is sincere—or at least he himself believes so. And that makes the deception being practiced on him all the crueler.

"Mains has been a busy man these past months, Watson—there is an old mill on his property, left to fall into ruin by his father but now, if word of mouth is to be believed, being prepared for a new lease on life. At least that is what the townsfolk would like to think—workmen, businessmen, metalworkers and tradesman have all been through this area in large numbers—along with an unspecified number of 'foreign types in leather coats that keeps themselves to themselves.' It is clear we have come to the right place—the hub of Mr. Mains' activities.

"All that remains now is to find the man himself, and extract the full story from him."

It sounded easy when Holmes put it so simply, but I was all too aware of the snowy landscape that needed to be traversed to reach our goal, never mind the peril that might face us on our arrival.

"Did no one remark on the ring?" I asked.

Holmes smiled.

"No one did. But they all saw it, and for a group that size not to have remarked on something this outlandish? Well, that is remarkable in itself, is it not?"

"They were hiding something from us?"

"Isn't everyone?" Holmes said, and laughed again. He seemed to be enjoying himself immensely.

The rabbit pie proved to be delicious and, washed down with some heady local ale, was quite the best possible antidote to our ordeal on the train. We were quite content to finish our evening sitting by the inn's large fireplace, all thought of our hardships of the previous night fading into memory.

"You asked in the train about the 'end-game', Watson," Holmes said over a last pipe before retiring to bed. "Well, I feel we are getting closer by the minute. It is our move now — we had best make sure it is a decisive one."

14

There was no more snow overnight, but it had been bitterly cold, and in the town at least, the streets were rutted with ice as hard as stone. My hopes of getting a driver were low, but I was to be surprised at the second time of asking when the man agreed to take us—at least as far as the carriage would pass—along the hillside road to Mains' property.

I was also surprised to find that Holmes had ordered a small travelling hamper of food from the landlord of the inn.

"We may be abroad for longer than we would like. It is best to be prepared."

At nine o' clock sharp, having eaten another hearty breakfast, we were on our way. It was a crisp clear morning, and the snow-covered views across the Border valleys were as stunning as any Afghani mountains could ever be. The carriage traveled at a fair trot along the side of the hills for a very pleasant half an hour during which I almost felt cozy. Holmes sat opposite me, lost in thought, puffing on a pipe. It was a most pleasant way to spend a winter morning.

It was not to last. I heard the horses neigh and whinny up front, the driver shouted a one-word command, and the carriage came to an abrupt halt that almost threw me into Holmes' lap.

"This is as far as I can go, sirs," the driver's voice called down to us.

"I can pay more," Holmes said. "Just name your price."

"It's not a question of the money, sir—have a look for yourself."

We disembarked, a chill breeze immediately biting at my cheeks, and saw the reason for the abrupt end to our ride. The narrow road ahead had been blocked by a wall of snow some four feet high, drifting across the full width and banked high up the side of the hill.

"There is no way round?" I asked.

The driver shook his head.

"There's just enough room for me to turn and go back as it is. The Mains Mill, and the big house, are at the far end of this valley—about four miles on—and this is the only way in or out."

"Shank's pony it is, then," Holmes said, although he did not look in the slightest bit daunted by the prospect.

I retrieved the food hamper—thankfully it was made in such a way that it could be strapped across one's back, and I took the first carry. We said our thanks to the driver and had a smoke while we watched him delicately and ever so carefully maneuver the carriage and horses in a series of small movements that culminated with him facing back along the road to Hawick.

"Are you sure I cannot take you back, sirs?" he said. "The weather can turn fast up here."

"We have come this far," Holmes said. "I am certain we can manage another four miles."

The driver nodded.

"I shall pass out word that you're on the road," he said. "Just in case. Whatever you do, do not stray off the path—you'll only find a quick way to Hell at this time of year."

And with that he was off and away. For a time we heard the rattle and clatter of wheels on rutted ice, and then we were left in silence. The only sounds came from a cold breeze whistling in our ears and the crunch of snow underfoot as we walked up to the snow bank and surveyed the full scale of our next obstacle.

"Come on, Watson," Holmes said, and scrambled up to the top of the drift. He turned away from me and looked up the valley towards our destination. "There is about twenty yards of this; thereafter, it looks as if our path might be a bit clearer."

It proved to be a long twenty yards, most of it spent thigh-deep in soft snow, struggling to move more than a few inches forward with each step. At one point I sank in so far—almost chest deep, that Holmes had to bodily drag me out to stop me being engulfed. By the time I was finally able to push through to stand on road again rather than snow, I was cold to the bone and already dog-tired. The prospect of four miles of the same filled me with nothing but dread.

I let Holmes carry the hamper for a while after that, but even without the added weight, it was a tiresome uphill slog that faced us for the rest of the morning. Even Holmes showed some signs of fatigue when we finally reached the head of the valley, turned a sharp bend in the road, and got our first look at the Mains grounds.

Had I not been quite so weary, I might have enjoyed the view more. We had reached the end of the narrow valley, and the Mains ancestor who had built the imposing house on a high outcrop could not have chosen a more commanding position. The house itself was mainly made up of two tall turrets of gray stone in the Scottish baronial style, and stood tall, looking over the whole length of the valley into the snow-covered hills in the distance. Lower down the slope on the banks of a fast-moving stream sat a squat sandstone building—nowhere near as handsome in appearance, but almost twice the size of the house above, and built for business rather than aesthetics. Three red brick chimneys rose from its southern end, and a cluster of smaller buildings I took to be dwelling houses for the workers clung along the edge of the far side of the valley from us.

We seemed to be the only people in the area—everything was quiet and still, the snow unbroken as far as the eye could see.

"What now, Holmes?"

"Let us find a convenient spot, and spy out the lie of the land," he said, and ushered me off the road and behind a trio of tall pines. We found an overhanging rock we could both sit under in relative shelter from the elements, and my overcoat provided almost adequate protection for our rears against the cold seeping from the ground. We had a clear view of both the house and the mill, and settled in for a wait.

By the time we had been there for almost two hours, I was feeling the cold in my bones again, and there had been no movement apart from a solitary dog fox that took one look in our direction and immediately fled the opposite way. Holmes lit up a smoke. I joined him, and we cracked open the hamper to find a most welcome array of sandwiches, cold pies and two bottles of ale. I would have preferred something hot, but the ale was strong and heady and did much to improve my mood.

After eating, we had another smoke, and then Holmes stood.

"There is clearly no one home," Holmes said. "Or if they are, they are keeping their heads down. Let us go and rattle a few cages, shall we?"

"Anything to get out of this blasted cold," I replied.

We stowed the hamper under the overhang, closing it securely lest the dog fox became curious, and walked, in open view, along the short stretch of road towards the main entrance to the house.

I felt the weight of the service pistol in my pocket, and consider having it in hand, but Holmes seemed relaxed, for the moment at least, and there was nothing to give any indication that we were in any immediate danger. We made fresh footprints along the length of the snow-covered pathway as we approached the tall oak door.

The bell was a very old pulley-and-rope affair, and the sound of its ringing seemed to echo inside the house.

No one answered. Holmes pulled the rope for a second ring, longer this time.

"It's a long way back before we reach a warm bed and some rabbit stew," I said, thinking more about having to traverse the deep snowdrift for a second time.

Just as I was resigning myself to an arduous walk, the tall door swung open in front of us, smoothly and without a sound, as if recently oiled.

"At least we will not have to sneak in through the kitchen this time," Holmes said, and stepped forward. I walked through the doorway to stand beside him, and the door swung shut, just as noiselessly, behind us.

The house—I hesitate to call it that, as it was more in the way of a small castle—felt warm and slightly musty. It also felt lived-in—I cannot put it any better than that, but I knew for a certainty that we were not alone. I believe Holmes felt something of the same; he was noticeably more tense as we made our way through the high vaulted hallway.

A voice, hardly more than a croak, called out from a doorway to our left.

"Through here, gentlemen," it said. "I have been waiting for you."

We walked through into a library, although this one was on a far grander scale than in Mains' London property, being two stories high with an ironwork balcony all around just above head level, the oak shelves stacked full with leather-bound tomes of great antiquity. Three armchairs were arranged around a small fire that was completely dwarfed by a massive stone grate with a high handsome mantel that looked like polished granite and must have weighed a ton.

Mains sat in one of the chairs. At first I did not recognize him, for his health had deteriorated markedly in the short time since our last meeting, giving him the appearance of a man twice his age, shrunken inside a wool suit many sizes too large for his frame. Open sores wept on his scalp beneath thinning strands of hair that were all that remained of his luxurious oiled locks. His eyes were moist and rheumy, red-rimmed and sunk in graying pits far back in his face. He raised a hand and I saw the veins and muscles through skin almost as transparent as glass.

"Good God, man," I said, my medical training overcoming any reticence I might have felt. "What has become of you?"

I moved forward toward him, but he waved me away, rather feebly, and only with an effort that seemed to tire him further.

"Please sit," he said. "There is Scotch on the table if you wish, but little else in the way of sustenance, I'm afraid—I am past the need of it. Sit, and I will tell you the story you have come to hear—if I am given the time to finish it."

Holmes did the honors, pouring us each two fingers of

peat-colored malt I could not identify, but which proved to be fiery and smooth in equal measure and went down very nicely, doing much to dispel the memory of the morning cold. Mains waited until we were settled and then began to speak, his voice only just carrying above the crackle and spit of the logs on the fire.

"I like to think of myself as something of a visionary," he began. "It is why they chose me.

"My company is the best at what we do because I employ the best. I actively seek out the new and revolutionary and put it to work. My boats have the latest engines and the newest hull designs, my cargoes have the most efficient refrigeration and storage techniques known to science, and I employ a specially selected team of researchers whose only job is to find innovative ways to make my company bigger, stronger—and wealthier.

"I believe it was this very forward-looking state of mind that drew them to me in the first place. They made themselves known to me in late August—here in this very room. I was going over the blueprints for a new storage facility in the Amazon basin when he appeared to me—you know the man I mean; you saw him yourself in St. Columba's.

"As you can imagine, it came as something of a shock, and at first, like Holmes, I suspected trickery—a man in my position gets much attention from people intent on relieving me of some of my money. But he showed me wonders, this Londoner who had taken a leap of faith and been rewarded with the stars.

"His story was of a mind unfettered by the bounds of Earth, and a race of people who have watched us from afar for millennia but now feel it is their duty to save us from war and disaster—to save us from ourselves."

I almost interjected at that point. I have seen enough of war to know that it is brutal and ugly—and that many of our fellow men revel in its beats and rhythms. You cannot save those that do not want to be saved. I held my peace—for the time being, even as Mains paused, and coughed into a handkerchief that was quickly stained red. To my trained eye it was obvious: something was eating away inside him, an advanced consumption that must be burning through him like wildfire. He was not long for this world.

"The Londoner asked for my help in his quest," Mains continued after a pause to gather his strength. "And I gave it gladly, sending telegrams out to garner support in the ports where my cargoes were gathered and where my ships visited. In a matter of weeks, we had a cadre of like-minded individuals, meeting across the world, organizing in the background, making the way ready. And now our work shall bear fruit. Things are almost in place."

"In place for what, may I ask?" Holmes asked. He had sat silently so far, his gaze never leaving Mains' face.

"It is almost time for the revealing," Mains said. He smiled, but that merely brought on a fresh coughing fit that left him even weaker than before. "An event has been planned that will change the world and end war forever—we will usher in a time when we will become students at the feet of new teachers."

Holmes snorted.

"You are not an idealist, man—you're a naïve fool. And tell me—apart from the man we all saw in the church—have you seen these so-called teachers of yours?"

"Not yet—the time is not right, and when they come we will have …"

Holmes waved him away.

"Yes, yes—a new, better, tomorrow—that has been the promise of the strong to the weak since time began. The weak are still waiting. I have heard more than enough to know they will be waiting for a while to come. Tell me one more thing, Mr. Mains—did these new teachers of yours ask you anything else? Did they, for example, ask you to seek out anyone in particular?"

Mains grinned—without the accompanying cough this time.

"Yes, indeed. I knew you would be the one to see that. They asked me to find extraordinary minds—and I have been doing so—have done so—and now we have one of the most extraordinary of all right where we want him. Welcome to the future, Mr. Holmes."

Holmes sprang to his feet.

"It's a trap, Watson."

Mains smiled as a vibration started up around us, the library resonating as if we were inside some great bell. Books shuddered in position on the shelves, and the rugs seemed to dance lightly on the floorboards as the hum grew louder, more insistent. Holmes turned towards the door, effort clearly visible in his face as he strained and tried to push against some unseen force. The hum rose in pitch, and then rose again, a banshee screeching in my head, a banshee with a hammer that pounded behind my eyes until I could endure it no more.

I fell away into a mercifully silent darkness.

15

I woke to a blinding light in my eyes and a distant hum that was all too reminiscent of the one I had fled my senses to leave behind. It was several seconds before my sight adjusted and I was able to take in my surroundings, and when I did so I half-thought I was still unconscious, still in the throes of a fevered dream.

I was securely tied, hands behind me, roped to a tall metal column—a support stanchion, and one of many that ran in a twin row along the length of the building away from me. I knew exactly where we were—three brick kilns dominated the far end of the old mill, and the sandstone of the main walls of the building was most distinctive. The composition of the interior, however, was another matter entirely. The space was full of shining metal and sparkling crystal, a bewildering array of objects—obviously mechanical—whose purpose I could not even begin to discern. High above, the whole mill was lit by two large shining globes of white light that seemed to hover without support a yard or so below the rafters of the ceiling.

The vibration was coming from the metal and glass contraptions—lights pulsed and static cracked, sending a short burst of blue sparks running up one wall before dissipating in the rafters.

Holmes was tied to the next stanchion in sequence to my right. He smiled thinly when he saw I was awake.

"Welcome to the future, Watson," he said, and motioned

with his head that I should look to my left. Someone stood there with his back to me, bent over a long table, obviously intent on some task. It took me a second to realize it was not even remotely human.

It was the size of a grown man, but looked more like a hideous shrimp. The body was segmented and chitinous like that of a crustacean, but this was no marine creature—it had membranous wings. The wings were currently tucked tightly against its back, giving it a hunched appearance, and judging by the size of the hunch, they would be adequate to lift its weight into powered flight—and more than large enough to look almost like a leather coat when pulled around the body.

There were no arms or hands to speak of; I counted four pairs of limbs. The pair the thing used as legs—I use the word loosely here—were more stout and thicker than the rest, each being tipped with three horny claws extended to balance its weight at the front while a segmented tail completed the tripod behind it. I knew now what had made the bird-like markings we had observed in the crypt, the church, and outside the railway carriage.

The other appendages looked more flexible and nimble, and as I watched, the thing leaned forward and delicately picked up a tool from the table. It turned slightly as it did so, and for the first time I got a good look at its face—or rather lack of one. Instead of features, there was only a mound of ridged flesh, pale and greasy, like a mushroom towards the end of its cycle. A multitude of thin snake-like appendages wafted around its head, and I took these to be the equivalent of sensory organs, although quite how they might function, I had no idea. There was also a scar down the whole left side of the ridged flesh, and when I smelled vinegar, I knew where Holmes' alkali had struck it.

I also knew what the thing was doing—it was preparing for surgery. Mains lay on the table beneath it, naked as the day he was born, his head completely shaved in readiness for what was to come. He was fully conscious. He saw me looking, and smiled.

"Now you will see the glory that is waiting," he said. "I will show you the way to a future without fear."

I have no idea what form of alien science accomplished what happened next—it is a procedure far beyond the skill of any medicine with which I am familiar. Within seconds, and with only a few deft strokes of a tool that seemed to cut and cauterize in the same movement, the back of Mains' skull was laid open. The creature took up another tool and made a long slit down the length of the backbone. To my further amazement and wonder, the man was still fully conscious throughout, and showed no sign of pain or even discomfort.

"Goodbye, Holmes" he said, and smiled. "I shall see you on the other side."

The crustacean—for that was how I thought of it—moved aside to fetch a tall cylindrical jar of glass and silver. Mains winked at me; the creature leaned forward and, using three limbs at once, tugged in a single sharp movement, swiftly lifting and turning to drop the detached brain and spinal column as a bloody mess into the jar, where it floated in a thick fluid, as if suspended there. Mains' body jerked, just once, and then slumped—stone dead without the controlling influence of his senses.

There was more to come: the creature lifted the jar—which must have weighed several stone at least—and carried it to a long metal wall. With a wave of a limb, a door slid silently open to reveal a shelf running almost the whole length of the mill, stacked tightly with more of the tall jars, each of which had a brain and spinal column floating inside like some mutant jellyfish.

Within seconds of Mains' brain being added to the line, a misty haze of dancing light filled the space before us. It seemed to come from everywhere yet nowhere, accompanied by a distant hum. I knew what was coming—we'd seen this before, in the ruin of St. Columba's. The light and color coalesced and thickened, hanging into a similar flattened oval to the one we'd seen in the church. The surface dulled to a flat gray, and a new image formed—a head, out of focus at first and then sharpening to clarity. Mains' smiling face looked straight at us. He had lost all hint of illness, and now looked like the healthy man we had met in London. He spoke, echoing his earlier words.

"Welcome to the future."

The face turned to look at Holmes.

"Pure intellect, unburdened by the day-to-day need for sustenance, untainted by the filth and grime of modern living—no need for conflict or strife—an end to war. Imagine it, Holmes."

"Oh, I can imagine it all too well," Holmes said. "And so can these creatures you call your teachers. Tell me—how do they plan to convince those without the benefit of your new freedom that this is the future? A glass jar for every man, woman and child on the planet? That is hardly a strong case for change, is it?"

"They have a demonstration in mind," Mains said. "A new power source myself and my research team have been working on alongside them—something that will make coal, gas, even electricity obsolete—free power, for all."

Holmes spoke quietly.

"And tell me—were you sick at all before you began working on this new power?"

I caught a movement at the corner of my eye; I looked over at Holmes and then quickly away again lest my glance was noticed—he was attempting to loosen his bonds, and had indeed almost got one hand free.

"Join me, Holmes—the Mi-Go can take us away, show us the stars; we can travel out and meet our destinies."

"I fear you have been misled," Holmes said. "They intend to use you for their own purposes—such is often the way of the strong when the weak capitulate. And this time, I shall prove it to you."

Holmes shouted, his voice ringing through the room.

"John Green? Are you here? It is Holmes, John. Help me understand."

A new oval coalesced in the air beside the first, and John Green's face looked out at us.

"Mr. Holmes? Is that you? It's proper dark in here—I can't rightly see you. Have you come to take me home? This was nice for a while, but my poor Jean will be beside herself if I ain't home soon."

Holmes had his right hand free now, and was working quickly on the left.

"We can't go. Not quite yet, John. Tell me—have you seen this demonstration that Mains is expecting? Can you show me the details?"

"Certainly, Mr. Holmes, sir," John said. "It's some kind of bomb and …"

Mains screamed.

"That is a lie. It is a power source—freedom from slavery."

The alien creature had not remained idle during this exchange—it moved to one of the crystal-and-metal contraptions—a twenty-foot long tube of silver, brass, and glass coils. I had no idea how it might work, but I immediately knew I was looking at a weapon. The crustacean made some movements above the metal and crystal tube with the clawed appendages that seemed to pass for hands. It spoke, alternately hissing and guttural, completely unintelligible to my ears. But the meaning was clear enough as a three-dimensional image formed in the air above the weapon—the well-known outline of the Thames at Westminster, the Houses of Parliament bathed in sunshine.

"Do you see?" Holmes said, turning to Mains. "They mean to destroy London—there's your demonstration."

Mains looked close to tears.

"I would never ..."

Holmes broke free of his bonds and strode to stand face to face with the oval images.

"Show me," he said to Green.

Green's face wavered and disappeared, to be replaced by a desert scene, one that quickly turned to a flash of light so bright I had to avert my eyes. When I looked back a cloud hung over the desert—a tall mushroom-stalked cloud rising high above a fireball that consumed everything in its path.

Holmes looked grim. "And this is what they plan for London?"

Green's face reappeared. "I ain't thought about it that way afore now, Mr. Holmes—you know me and connections—but I suppose it must be. Can I go home now?"

Green seemed more like a lost child than a man with a brain as magnificent as that described by Holmes, and I believed I knew why.

"His brain is stagnating, Holmes—these jars are only temporary—they will never sustain the mind for very long. A brain needs a body as much as a body needs a brain."

"That is not true," Mains shouted. "I am free—they promised."

The creature passed a hand over the long tube again, causing it to glow and throb, a vibration that rose quickly louder, sending a new hum through the mill. Fine dust was dislodged from the rafters to fall around us, and the globes of light seemed to tremble and fade before flaring back into full life. The long tube glowed and thrummed, and the image of Westminster came into sharper focus.

Holmes leapt forward, in the same movement taking the syringe from his waistcoat pocket. The creature turned towards him. Holmes feinted left but went right, an old boxer's move I knew from my youth. The thing was no pugilist—Holmes got through a feeble attempt at defense, plunged the syringe deep into the flesh—right around where an eye might be, if it had had one—and pushed the plunger.

The result was immediate—the creature fell in a heap to the ground, limbs thrashing wildly. Flesh sloughed and ran, hissing and bubbling in a noxious mess. The snake-like tentacles whipped and curled in frenzy before going still only seconds later. There was a last, moist, gurgle; then the top third of the thing fell apart in wet ooze. The tang of strong vinegar scorched my nasal passages.

Holmes kicked at the solid thorax remaining—there was no sign of movement.

He came over and untied me.

"I told you he would not best me another time."

I stepped free of my bonds and looked around. The glowing tube continued to throb, the vibration quickening and the hum steadily rising in intensity.

"I don't think we're out of the woods yet, old boy."

Mains grinned like a manic. "You see, Holmes—it is coming anyway. You cannot fight the future."

I had seen quite enough. I walked over to the cabinet and put my hands on the jar containing Mains' brain.

"Shut off the weapon," I shouted. "Stop it now, or so help me I will dash your brains all over this floor alongside your friend here."

"I cannot stop it," Mains said, still smiling. "Even should I want to, I do not know how."

Holmes had moved over to the weapon and was examining the long glass tube, but seemed at a loss as to how to proceed.

"If I could be of some help, Mr. Holmes," Green said, "I think I know how to do it—they've had me controlling all kinds of things for them—they said my brain was the best they'd seen for the job. I can do it—but it'll send this whole place to blazes if I do."

"Then do it, man!" Holmes said.

The image of London came into yet sharper focus, and grew, so that it seemed we were flying, ever faster, straight for the old clock tower itself.

"Do it now!" Holmes shouted.

"I ain't ever going home, am I, Mr. Holmes?" Green said, a great sadness showing on his features.

"I'm afraid not, old chap."

"Tell Jean I love her," Green said, the image fading. The glass cylinder began to screech like fingernails on a chalkboard. Flaring light pulsed so fast it hurt the eyes to look at it.

"She knows already," Holmes said softly, as Green's image dissolved and the vibration rose to deafening levels. "She's waiting for you."

The globes of light dropped like stones and smashed into glittering fragments of glass and crystal, leaving us in a dim gloom. Mains' image still hung in the air, and I still held the glass jar in my hands.

"Time to go, Watson!" Holmes shouted.

More dust fell from above and bricks loosened and tumbled from the walls as the old building shook and trembled. The weapon glowed blue and then white; then piercing silver I could not look at. Holmes had already turned to go.

"Take me with you!" Mains screamed.

I put the glass jar back on the shelf alongside the others. "You chose your own future," I said. "I cannot do it for you. And I believe Mr. Green would like some company on the journey."

I left the jar on the shelf and followed Holmes in making a run for the nearest exit. I looked over my shoulder one last time to see Mains' image dissolve and fade, just as a piece of roof timber fell on the shelf, knocking the jars over and sending all that was left of Mains flopping on the mill floor.

We made it out just in time, although even so, the force of the blast when it came was enough to knock us flying into a fortuitous snowdrift.

I spat out muddy slush from my mouth and turned to see the mill collapse in on itself, the brick chimneys the last to go as they tumbled down in a roaring cloud of dust and buried Mains' remains under a mound of brick and rubble.

16

I only started to make sense of it much later that night, back in the inn at Hawick.

It had taken us an hour to walk to a spot where we started to find signs of life, and another hour to get a ride back to town. Then there was the matter of finding somewhere to send telegrams, before finally making our way back to our rooms in the Queen's Head.

By late evening we received news that Mycroft had Mains' property sealed off, and a large military presence had moved in within hours of our report. The inn was buzzing with speculation, but most of that was directed at the town police force and councilmen, and Holmes and I were able to find a quiet corner beside a roaring fire and enjoy some much-needed ale and more of that fine rabbit stew in relative privacy.

Once I had sat back from the table and lit a well-earned smoke, I asked Holmes if he would not rather be back on the grounds, involved in the aftermath and helping Mycroft make some sense of what had just happened.

"No," he replied. "We caught our murderer—or murderers, for Mains himself confessed to being complicit. The rest is in Mycroft's domain now; it will require the power and vigilance of governments to keep watch lest the creatures attempt a return."

Holmes lit up a cheroot of his own and seemed disinclined to discuss the matter any further.

"But do you think it would have worked?" I asked. "Could they indeed have succeeded?"

Holmes seemed lost in thought, and I was about to push for an answer when he spoke softly, so that no one else in the bar could overhear.

"It is an interesting strategy, I'll give them that," Holmes said. "Using our desire for an end to conflict against us is a touch of genius."

"And what if they were sincere," I said, giving voice to a concern I'd been harboring for some time. "What if they genuinely only wanted to help?"

Holmes laughed softly.

"By threatening to blow up London? Actually, it was more than a threat—you saw that for yourself, Watson. And having us all live in glass jars? Their technology was surely advanced enough for them to know, as you did, that minds would degrade and decay over time. No, I'm afraid that some of our brightest and best were sorely duped."

We had finished our ale, and I went to the bar for another round. When I returned, Holmes was still in a pensive mood, and he had still not answered my question to my satisfaction.

"Might it have worked, though?" I asked again. "I mean, the threat of a single huge bomb—would it have been enough to stop all other bombs—or would that one bomb be so large that it would destroy us anyway?"

Holmes was quiet for the longest time before answering.

"I too have been pondering that question, Watson," he said. "And neither answer is entirely satisfactory. We may only know when we have to face a large enough threat, and I fear that time may be coming all too soon."

Holmes flicked the stub of his cheroot into the fire, where it flared for a second before burning out. "And when it happens, we really will have to choose which future we want to live in."

The Hackney Horror

Further Reading

If you enjoyed this, you might enjoy my Holmes collection THE QUALITY OF MERCY AND OTHER STORIES, and my novel SHERLOCK HOLMES: THE DREAMING MAN

I am a Scottish writer, now living in Canada, with over thirty novels published in the genre press and over 300 short story credits in thirteen countries.

I have books available from a variety of publishers including Dark Regions Press and Severed Press, and my work has appeared in a number of professional anthologies and magazines with recent sales to NATURE Futures, Penumbra and Buzzy Mag among others.

I live in Newfoundland with whales, bald eagles and icebergs for company and when I'm not writing I drink beer, play guitar and dream of fortune and glory.

Willie Meikle
williammeikle.com

Other Books By William Meikle

Novels

The S-Squad Series
Berserker
Crustaceans
Eldren: The Book of the Dark
Fungoid
Generations
Island Life
Night of the Wendigo
Ramskull
Sherlock Holmes: The Dreaming Man
Songs of Dreaming Gods
The Boathouse
The Creeping Kelp
The Dunfield Terror
The Exiled
The Green and the Black
The Hole
The Invasion
The Midnight Eye Files: The Amulet
The Midnight Eye Files: The Sirens
The Midnight Eye Files: The Skin Game
The Ravine
The Valley
The Concordances of the Red Serpent
Watchers: The Battle for the Throne
Watchers: The Coming of the King
Watchers: Culloden
The Road Hole Bunker Mystery

Dagger of the Martyrs (With Steven Savile)
Hound of Night / Veil Knights #2 (as Rowan Casey)

NOVELLAS

Broken Sigil
Clockwork Dolls
Pentacle
Professor Challenger: The Island of Terror
Sherlock Holmes: Revenant
The House on the Moor
The Job
The Midnight Eye Files: Deal or No Deal
The Plasm
The CopyCat Murders
Tormentor

SHORT STORY COLLECTIONS

Carnacki: Heaven and Hell
Carnacki: The Edinburgh Townhouse
Carnacki: The Watcher at the Gate
Dark Melodies
Myth and Monsters
Professor Challenger: The Kew Growths
Samurai and Other Stories
Sherlock Holmes: The Quality of Mercy
The Ghost Club
Home From the Sea
Into The Black
Flower of Scotland
Augustus Seton: Collected Chronicles

Bug Eyed Monsters

Details of all of these works and more can be found at his website at **williammeikle.com**

Printed in Great Britain
by Amazon